John Lanne Buchanan

A Defence of the Scots Highlanders, in General

And some learned characters, in particular: With a new and satisfactory account of

the Picts, Scots, Fingal, Ossian, and his poems: as also, of the Macs, clans, Bodotria.

And several other particulars

John Lanne Buchanan

A Defence of the Scots Highlanders, in General
And some learned characters, in particular: With a new and satisfactory account of the Picts, Scots, Fingal, Ossian, and his poems: as also, of the Macs, clans, Bodotria. And several other particulars

ISBN/EAN: 9783337394080

Printed in Europe, USA, Canada, Australia, Japan

Cover: Foto ©Andreas Hilbeck / pixelio.de

More available books at **www.hansebooks.com**

A

DEFENCE

OF THE

SCOTS HIGHLANDERS,

IN GENERAL;

AND

SOME LEARNED CHARACTERS,

IN PARTICULAR:

With a new and fatisfactory Account of the

PICTS, SCOTS, FINGAL, OSSIAN, AND HIS POEMS:

As alfo,

Of the MACS, CLANS, BODOTRIA.

And

Several other Particulars refpecting the High Antiquities
of *Scotland.*

By the Rev. JOHN LANNE BUCHANAN.

LONDON:

Printed for J. EGERTON, Whitehall; W. STEWART,
Piccadilly; and W. RICHARDSON, Royal Exchange.

MDCCXCIV.

THE MARQUIS OF HUNTLY.

MY LORD,

THAT I fhould be equally fond and
proud of the honour of approaching
your Lordfhip in this manner cannot be ac-
counted fingular, feeing it is well known,
that your great name will adorn and raife the
reputation of any book to which it is prefixed;
more efpecially when your youth and fweetnefs of difpofition, which have made you
no lefs amiable, than your noble birth
have made you great, are alfo confidered.
On that acount, I humbly acknowledge,
that, by offering it, I do not at all compli-
ment your Lordfhip; much lefs do I court
the publick into a good opinion of myfelf,

a 2   having

having a much nobler motive than that interefted one: but I do, from humanity and
juftice, a tribute due to truth, attempt to
vindicate my country and people, who have
been illiberally infulted by the intemperate
rage of an unprovoked enemy, and prefume
to lay a fhort vindication of their character
before your Lordfhip, in hopes it will meet
with your countenance, both from the conftant regard which your noble anceftors ever
had, and the firm confidence your Lordfhip
has all along manifefted in favour of the
Scots in general, and Highlanders in particular. This princely mark of efteem is expected from a perfonage of your exalted rank;
and being at the fame time the reprefenta-
tive of a noble family, which, in point of
power and antiquity, is equalled by few,
and furpaffed by none in North Britain; I
fay, this mark of efteem and attention cannot fail of being highly pleafing to a brave
people,

people, who had the advantage of being
born and brought up under its influence,
and in its near vicinity, where their prowefs
have been tried, and their virtue amply re-
warded by the generous hand that led them
forth to action in the hour of danger,

To you, then, my Lord, thefe martial inhabitants naturally look up for patronage and
protection, when unjuftly and fo foully ca-
lumniated with fo much unmerited abufe and
obloquy, more particularly as your Lordfhip is
Prefident of the Highland Caledonian Society in London; gentlemen who alfo contribute liberally to encourage their country-
men to make progrefs in the feveral kinds
of improvement and refinement of manners.
I fhall only farther obferve, that I feel myfelf moved by inclination, and encouraged
by gentlemen of eminence, to dedicate the
following performance to the entertainment

of

of your leifure hours; and it is hoped that the variety and novelty contained therein will render it equally agreeable as intereſt-ing. Theſe confiderations, I flatter myſelf, will obtain pardon, for what otherwiſe would be confidered as a piece of vanity and preſumption.

I have the honour to be, with profound reſpect,

MY LORD,

Your Lordſhip's moſt obedient,

And moſt humble Servant,

JOHN LANNE BUCHANAN.

IT is hardly neceſſary to make an apology for the ſtyle of the enſuing ſheets. The ſubjeＣt of them excludes every thing of ſtudied elegance, or ornament of language ; all that can be looked for in them is plainneſs and perſpicuity ; both which it has been my greateſt pains to endeavour after as much as poſſible. If in theſe I have ſucceeded ſo as to pleaſe the ſenſible reader, the objeＣt of my wiſh is obtained ; and it is hoped the more candid of them will charitably excuſe whatever errors may have inadvertently dropt from my pen, on account of the ſincerity and honeſty of my intentions.

ADVERTISEMENT.

A Subject that is new and ſtriking, generally attracts the minds of men; and
judgment is freely paſſed upon it, as the in-
quiſitive ſpectators are more or leſs affected
by the object expoſed to their view. If the
narrative is probable, and fortunately clothed
with a pleaſing garb, then it gains credit and
admirers; if otherwiſe, the ſubject becomes
doubtful or inſipid, and gradually ſinks into
its original obſcurity. How far the following attempt, to throw light on a ſubject
which has hitherto been looked upon as a
kind of fable, will merit the firſt or laſt of
theſe deciſions, is by the Author left to ſtand
or fall by the judgment of the impartial
Public, before whom it is now to make its
appearance. He only has to ſay for himſelf, that his ſole aim is, if poſſible, to ſnatch
from oblivion, and bring into repute, cir-
cumſtances which to him appeared to have
been miſunderſtood and neglected, in ſpite of

B   the

the living language of an ancient people, that plainly indicate their having had an exift-ence. Yet the many able and learned gentle-men, who from age to age have laboured to do honour to their country, have unfor-tunately been ftrangers to the language, and refted fecure upon the authorities handed down by the old Greeks and Romans, as to infallible ftandards of appeal, though it is beyond a doubt that their own knowledge of the fubject was but extremely imperfect, and their information from fecond-hand be-hoved to be limited, or at beft but mifin-formed authority.—This affertion is mani-feft from their very inaccurate account of the geography of North Britain, as well as from the forced garb in which the Gaelic terms adopted by thefe ftrangers appear in print, when compared with their original manufcripts. Their looks and founds are fo extremely foreign and antiquated, that even a knowing accurate judge of the Celtic requires great exertions of his fkill to ftrip them of their exotic mafks, in order to make them intelligible. This is particularly

larly the cafe with regard to Fingal, Offian,
the Picts, Scots, Bodotria, Grampiani Montes, Ocelli Montes, and many more, which
the Greeks and Romans have ftript of their
original purity, by tranfpofitions of letters in
the middle, and taking from and adding
letters to their terminations, purely to make
them found agreeable to their own ears;
without once reflecting that a language
fo tortured was rendered unintelligible to
the natives, and which they could not apply any longer to the different objects to
which in its natural drefs it was fitly adapted: while the new-modelled expreffions
were left quite inapplicable to any one proper and fignificant object, to fatisfy a refined ear, and a real judge of that Celtic
tongue, to which thefe ftrangers had applied them. Of this the Author, without
vanity, thinks himfelf a competent judge,
as that language was familiar to him from
his infancy, and alfo from the line of his profeffion, he was under a neceffity of improv-
ing in it, both as it is fpoken in the Eaft and
Weft of Scotland. This, with a liberal

courfe

courfe of education, and the additional advantages he now poffeffes, of reading the different opinions of fuch authors as have touched on the high antiquities of Britain, place it within his power to elucidate the fubject in fuch a manner as he flatters himfelf will not only do it juftice, but render it entertaining, if not edifying to the reader.

He only regrets his own inferiority to the many able authors who have handled the fubject, though unfortunately their ignorance of the Celtic has difqualified them from giving that fatisfaction which their fuperior abilities would otherwife have yielded to the Public, and the honourable point of view in which they would have placed their country and its ancient language throughout all Europe.

If the Author might indulge himfelf with the hope that the following fpecimen of his knowledge in the Gaelic language would give any degree of fatisfaction to the judicious reader, he afterwards would enlarge more fully, by making a gloffary on many

more

more of the unknown terms ufed by authors, concerning the high antiquities of Great Britain,—fuch as Alabin, Britain, Caledc-nians, Vecturiones, Celts, Gaels, Attacotti, Mæatti, Ireland, Thule, Caffiterides, Trino-bantes, Ludgate, &c. all of them well known to belong to the antiquities of the Celts.

He expects indulgence from the judicious reader refpecting his early and almoft un-known account of the ancient inhabitants of the Ifles, and believes that his authori-ties will defend him from the lafh of the critics, more efpecially as he arrogates no praife to himfelf, and is only forry that his abilities did not equal his fincere defire to do more ample juftice to a fubject worthy of an abler pen.

Though the Author followsMr.Pincarton, he advertifes the reader, that it is not folely with a view to defend the injured High-landers and Learned Characters which fell under that gentleman's wrath, as he himfelf hath fufficiently fecured them from danger, from his own intemperate and unprovoked rage, and has fufficiently damned the credi-

B 3   bility

bility of his own works. And while the Macpherfons defpife the performance, and look on it as unworthy of an anfwer, much more ought the Author fo to do, being lefs concerned. But in regard Mr. Pincarton has handled the Picts, and other fubjects to which he is a ftranger, fo the Author improves the opportunity of following, and, if poffible, of convincing that enraged gentleman of his miftaken opinion of the Highlanders, and of fome Learned Characters with whom he has ufed too much freedom; and at the fame time he will endeavour to illuftrate a few of thefe epithets that have hitherto laboured under a kind of mift, and make them affume an appearance that will be at leaft new, and perhaps entertaining; and he hopes they will be fortunate enough to meet with the approbation of the impartial public—efpecially of the Learned, where the nature of the fubject leads him to make critical remarks, which, though neceffary, is but a dry theme, and of courfe lefs pleafant than a plain fmooth narrative, when no interruption is made to intercept the rapid career of the more fuperficial reader.

D E-

D E F E N C E

SCOTCH HIGHLANDERS.

AFTER reading an enquiry into the Hiftory of Scotland, written by Mr. John Pincarton, and confidering the afperity of that author, with the injurious, unfupport-ed, and illiberal reflections thrown out againft the Highlanders in general, and Learned Characters in particular; I was prompted to make a few remarks on his acrimony a-gainft them, and to ftate facts in their true light, as far as confifts with my own know-ledge, and thefe fupported by the authority of gentlemen of veracity and candour, in favour of the injured country and people fo *outrageoufly infulted.*

B 4   This

This fmall teftimony is a tribute due to Truth, and a duty which every man of honour ought to pay her. The writer, though not a native of the abufed fpot, had neverthelefs full accefs of knowing both the genius and difpofitions of the different claffes of people that inhabit thefe diftant regions.

But in order to do juftice properly to fo tender a fubject, as characters whether taken in a general or more limited point of view, it will be neceffary to follow Mr. Pincarton in a few particulars, by way of giving a fpecimen of his fpirit; for to attempt a commentary on the whole of his works would require two volumes, and even then but difguft my readers. And fhould not this fturdy aggreffor be convinced of his error, a circumftance *(as it is thought)* beyond hope, yet the Author flatters himfelf that the impartial Public will lend a favourable ear to a plaufible narrative, and fully fraught with veracity, offered by one who had no other motive but an honeft regard for truth.

From this gentleman's enquiry it appears, that

that he has a defign to obtrude the Gothic
Piks from Scandinavia upon the Scotch
nation, as anceſtors to the Pechs of North
Britain : yet as the two Macpherſons, Dr.
John, miniſter of Slate, in Skye, in his Critical Diſſertation, and Mr. James Macpherſon,
in his Introduction to the Hiſtory of Great
Britain and Ireland, have effectually blocked
up their entrance ; ſo Mr. Pincarton, who
has written poſterior to them, muſt firſt de-
ſtroy their credit, before he can open a free
paſſage for the Goths, his favourite people :
but his abuſing a whole nation of people,
learned and illiterate, for their ſakes, appears
unhandſome and inhumane ; however, of this
the reader will judge for himſelf.

———————

‘ CAMBDEN, both the Welch Llhyds,
‘ Innes, with the two Macpherſons, and
‘ others, maintain that the Picts were Celts,
‘ and Mr. Pincarton inſiſts that they were
‘ Goths, and ſpake the Gothic tongue, the
‘ parent of the preſent German, Daniſh,
‘ and Engliſh ; but if they were Celts, they
‘ would ſpeak the Camerag Celtic tongue.’

Here

Here he betrays his ignorance, in faying that the Celtic language is the fame with the Cumerag or Welch; they were not the fame in Cæfar's days, nor fince, nor at prefent, and they were but lately arrived in Britain before that time. Where, then, and when did they fpeak the fame language with the Scotch? Even the Llhyds grant that the Welch is not the original language of Britain, but the language fpoke by the Aborigenes, who were drove back to North Britain by the Britons from Belgæ.

Without enquiring critically into the truth of Mr. Pincarton's affertion, whether or not the Goths were anceftors to the Celts, feeing we know it is denied by men of learning and parts; yet we can affure the reader, that the Gaelic is as different from the Gothic language, as Greek is from Arabic. How far the Gaelic agrees with the Scots Englifh will appear, if any are curious of the experiment, from a fpeech carried on by any two men, one from each country, and each ignorant of the refpective tongue of the other; and whoever makes the trial will reap little edification from the dialogue,

As

As for the people called the Cumeras, their hiſtory is not only very dark, but it is extremely dubious whether ever ſuch lived in Scotland. At leaſt there are no veſtiges of their name left behind, to make it appear that they exiſted once there. The Cumera Iſles are ſpoken of by ſome as deriving their names from them, as alſo Comrie, and Mac-Gumbries; but the firſt of theſe take the name from the confluence or confluct of two ſtreams of ſea, the one from the Mull of Kintyre on the North Weſt, and the other from the Iriſh Channel and Iſle of Mann on the Eaſt, both ſtreams in the flux ruſhing violently into the mouth of the Clyde, and meeting at the two Iſles alluded to; *Co-ruidh* confluence, or *Corrag* a confliĉt, being the Gaelic name of ſuch junĉtions, and the Iſles very properly received their names from thence. As for Comrie pariſh in Perthſhire, it derives its name from the confluence of the rivers *Ruobuill* and Earn, which meet at the village of Comrie; and from thence many of the inhabitants receive their

their names, Comries and MacComries, or MontoGumbries, which are the fame people.

' The two Macpherfons, led by the fame
' wife Celtic ideas, defire we fhall in future
' know the Piƈts to be Gaels, of hur aun dear
' blud and bones: and they fay, Believe other-
' wife on your peril; for are not we fkilled
' in the old Celtic, and new in nonfenfe and
' non-entity? And what are Tacitus, and
' Ammianus, and Bede, and all the other old
' fools to us? Do not we know more than
' them? Are not we two wife men, and quite
' of a new fchool?'

One would expeƈt that this rhapfody would have been accompanied with quotations from Tacitus, &c. to lead us to examine and judge for ourfelves; yet not one, but becaufe thefe authors barely mention the name, without enquiring, or informing themfelves, whence their language was de-rived.

Therefore Mr. Pincarton affirms, that the two Macpherfons are in the wrong, though they knew the language in debate, and the

others

others in the right, though ſtrangers to it;
—ſtrange mode of forming concluſions !

Before he anſwers Cambden, Innes, &c.
theſe grave authors, who maintain that the
'Picts were Welch, that is, the Ancient Britons from Belgæ, he goes on to addreſs the
Macpherſons, as ſoon as laughter permits;
for, continues he, it is impoſſible to preſerve
one's muſcles when he meets with utter
abſurdity or ignorance in the garb of wiſdom and learning.

‘ The Doctor and Mr. Macpherſon aſſert,
‘ that the Scotch Highlanders are the real
‘ Caledonians, and the Picts a part of them,
‘ the former living on the Weſt, the latter
‘ living on the South and Eaſt ſide. Such
‘ opinions mark the decline of learning in
‘ Scotland, becauſe they are contradictory to
all authorities and facts.’ (Where are theſe
authorities and facts to be met with, except
the romantic intelligence of the Iriſh and
their followers ?)

‘ An ignorant writer will advance any
‘ opinion that will ſooth his ſickly fancy, or
‘ gratify his prejudice, becauſe he is ignorant
‘ of

' of the truth, ignorant of his danger, igno-
' rant of the contemptuous thoughts enter-
' tained of him by others. The opinions
' of the two Macpherfons are truly Celtic,
' foolifh, and ignorant in the extreme. Hea-
' ven forbid that a regular anfwer fhould be
' given them! fuch weak vifionaries as are
' five centuries behind the reft of mankind,
' and not fo knowing now, as Jeffrey of
' Monmouth, their brother, was in the
' twelfth century.

 ' The Cumeri actually poffeffed Scotland
' for centuries before the Picts came in. The
' names of rivers and mountains, &c. are
' perpetual; but the works of man, as cities,
' &c. are changeable.''

 The remarks of a certain Baronet on
the fcurrility of O'Connor, in a fimilar cafe,
againft James Macpherfon, are pretty applicable to the prefent, fo we fhall fuftain them
for a counterpoife, viz. '' That he has laid
afide good fenfe and argument for fcurrility
and perfonal abufe.'' It is, however, to be
hoped, continues he, that Mr. Macpherfon
will not honour it with a reply. Such an

illiberal

illiberal attack ! which is as impotent as it
is low and ungentlemanny. When a man
appears extremely angry upon a fubjeƈt,
which can only be fupported by a cool and
temperate difquifition, it is a conclufive argument, that he is fenfible of the weaknefs
of his caufe, or extremely diffident of his
own abilities to fupport it.

" But as the character of modefty is not
very confpicuous in Mr. O'Conner's works,
it would feem to me, that his intemperate
rage proceeds from a narrow and irafcible
fpirit, thrown into confufion by the difco-
very made by Mr. Macpherfon of the Mi-
lefian fyftem."—Nor is it unlikely but the
fpirit of Mr. Pincarton was thrown into
fome deranged ftate of confufion by the
fame Mr. Macpherfon and others, by their
giving a probable account of the Scots Pechs,
different from the fcheme given by him of
the Norwegian Piks. But as the gentleman,
for his outrage againft the whole nation,
deferves an appellation which may not drop
from the pen of a decent writer, the generous reader may, if he pleafes, caft away
the

the libel, though the abundance of unpleafant facts will adhere to his memory.

- We obferved above, that the Cumeræ or Welch, or Britons, according to Cambden and other Welch hiftorians, came to Great Britain but a few centuries before Cæfar's time; yet Mr. Pincarton, without authority, will place them in Great Britain many centuries before the Picts, who are faid by fome to have arrived about 300 years before Chrift, as imagined only, but on ftrict enquiry, a grofs miftake; and as no author of character, before Mr. Pincarton, has ever attempted to publifh in oppofition to the fentiments of the Macpherfons on that head, why might not they eftablifh fo plaufible, and I may add, fo true an opinion, efpecially as they were fupported by a living ancient language, and alfo guided by the names of rivers, mountains, ftraths, &c. the moft infallible of all guides, when no written authority could be found, feeing their thorough knowledge of the Celtic language, which gave them names originally, determined the fcale in their favour? and Mr.

Pincarton

Pinkerton had ferved his purpofe much better, had he fpared his ribaldry (of hur aun dear blud and bones), becaufe any fenfible reader will perceive malice at the bottom, and that their publications are written in a ftyle of Englifh language far fuperior to his own; for railing and reafoning are two diftinct things; and the moment a writer lofes fight of his temper, or defcends into fcurrilities, he defeats the very purpofe he wifhes to eftablifh.

Mr. Gibbons gives a different account of the Doctor's abilities. " Dr. Macpherfon, fays Mr. Gibbons, was a minifter in the Ifle of Skye; and it is a circumftance honourable to the prefent age, that a work fo replete with erudition and criticifm fhould have been compofed in the moft remote of the Hebrides."

This account in favour of the Doctor, by an author incomparably more elegant and able than Mr. P. is fufficient to wipe away the cruel infinuation againft the merit of that learned gentleman, by his unjuft comparifon.

The kind reader is defired to pardon the

C   following

following narrative and well-known fact, namely to inform him, that in the whole fhire of Invernefs, Gaelic is the vernacular tongue of the inhabitants, and fpoken there in the greateft purity ; and yet that the Englifh language is alfo fpoken there more properly than in any other fpot in N. Britain. This will appear lefs furprifing when it is confidered, that all fuch as fpeak it are taught at the firft feminaries of learning in Scotland ; and fuch as are of inferior rank, and in want of better opportunities, are more immediately taught from the mouths of thofe inftructed in it.

At Invernefs, in particular, there is an eminent fchool, endowed with a yearly falary of 60 or 70 pounds, for the maintenance of an able mafter ; and every gentleman whofe abilities entitle him to fuch a living, muft be acquainted with the moft approved modern authors, in order to put them into the hands of his pupils. Thefe authors are explained in a language as free from provinciality of dialect as poffible. Hence it happens that people from that quarter are better underftood in London,

than

than thofe from moft other parts of Scotland.

They muft be allowed, therefore, to be
almoft totally ignorant of the old Scotch
dialects, fo much ufed in common converfation among the vulgar in the South, where
Allan Ramfay and Capt. William Hamilton's
Collections of Old Scotticifms are fo generally run upon by that clafs of people.
How Mr. P. comes to fill the mouths of
the two Macpherfons with his own jargon,
a language unknown in Skye and Invernefs-
fhire, is a myftery he fhould explain to the
public. Truth ought to precede malignity,
with every fenfible writer; and certain it
is, that hur aun dear blud and bones are
not much known over thefe countries; fo
that Mr. P. may clap them into his pocket,
until a better opportunity to difpofe of them
to better advantage fall in his way.

 ‘ The reader will obferve, that it is a
‘ fingular quality of the Celtic tongue, to
‘ corrupt and debafe others to its own vague
‘ form, efpecially by altering the beginning
‘ of words, fo that it becomes as difficult to

‘ recognize

' recognize them, as to know a perſon in
' a maſk. A modern Engliſh word or name,
' when clothed in a Celtic habit, becomes
' as ſingular and old-like, as a real Celtic
' word of two thouſand years ſtanding.'

The Hebrews and old Egyptians contradict Mr. P. flatly, for they abuſe the modern
Greeks and Romans for their frequent uſe
of tranſpoſitions and variations of letters, as
well as for their additions to the beginnings and ends of words, which have ſo
mutilated and corrupted the ancient languages, as to render them quite unintelligible; while the Hebrews, Egyptians and
Celts have handed down their languages
unalterably the ſame in ſpelling and pronunciation; ſo that Mr. P. boldly reverſes
the well-known mode of ſpeaking and pro-
nouncing Gaelic, by making it wear a different maſk from reality.

But the Gaelic, like the Chineſe, is an original language, as may be inferred from the
ſmall number of words which it contains,
and which are, at leaſt many of them, mo-
noſyllables, as language at firſt naturally

eonſiſts

confifts of, almoft every word being a radix,
and in a great meafure free from many de-
clenfions, conjugations, moods and tenfes, of
which all other more modern languages are
more or lefs compounded. Gaelic is the
longeft preferved to this day, and is pretty
free from mixture and corruption, notwithftanding the difadvantages it had to ftruggle
with, from the ftrong attempts made to
deftroy it. And the reader may fafely believe, that any exotic word adopted of late
is well known to be foreign by the natives
who fpeak the language—though ftrangers
to that tongue and people would not expect
fo much difcernment among them.

Thus we may farther remark, that Jo-
fephus blames people for taking the liberty
of altering words, names, and terms of perfons and things to their own fancy, and
charges the Greeks with the practice of
changing names to tickle the ear, and carry
the word glibber off the tongue; but our
people, fays he, neither allow nor delight in
fuch things. The Greeks have turned Noe
into Noachos : but we keep by the fame fyl-

lable,

lable, and never vary the termination; as do
alfo the Celts *.

‘ The Welfh, and Piĉts, and Belgians, had
‘ their fhare in the Irifh tongue about the
‘ birth of Chrift,’ (from what authority pray?)
‘ but it is as difficult to recognize the foreign
‘ words in Irifh as in the Welfh, and more fo.’

But this man, though grofsly ignorant of
the Celtic tongue, marches on, in defiance
of fhame and authority, to perfuade his
Englifh reader that the Gaelic debafes all
other tongues, and ftamps age on modern
words, like a young man under an old
mafk : but, in return, we abfolutely deny it,
and challenge Mr. P. to bring forward a
few of thofe, and try his art, to impofe on
any one competent judge of the Celtic if
he can. On the contrary, the language requires no fuch auxiliaries to help people to
exprefs their thoughts, as it has a fufficient
copia verborum of its own, and no lefs per-
tinent. The language, indeed, may be corrupted, and even loft altogether ; but fuch
alterations and extraneous materials are eafily

* Parfon's Remarks on the Antiquities of Japhet.

known,

known, as they are frequently little adapted
to the purpofe intended. The Welfh and Irifh
writers might lead Mr. P. to exprefs himfelf
fo unguardedly ignorant ; but no real Scotch
Highlander would believe him, or them.

‘ Some late fuperficial dreamers, conti-
‘ nues Mr. P. have afferted, that the Gaelic
‘ in Scotland, among the Highlanders, is
‘ the pureft dialect of the Celtic : this opi-
‘ nion was unhappily advanced by people
‘ who tell us, that poems yet repeated in the
‘ Highlands are in the fame words as in the
‘ third century. Au miracle ! au miracle !
‘ Immortal languages of the Greeks and Ro-
‘ mans, what are your glories to thefe ? All
‘ the eternal monuments of your authors
‘ could not fix the fpoken languages half fo
‘ long as that of thefe favages *has* ftood
‘ upon its own bottom — the favourite fpot
‘ where eternity has fixed its own neft for *its*
‘ own phœnix.’

‘ Among the mountains of Scotland, the
‘ mutability of human affairs has no power.
‘ No doubt a Celtic underftanding will be al-
‘ ways a Celtic underftanding; and that folly

C 4   ‘ imputed

' imputed by the Greeks and Romans to the
' Celts, remains unimpaired ; but this Gaelic
' of the Highlanders is undoubtedly more
' corrupt than either the Welſh or Iriſh.'

Paul Pezeron flatly contradicts Mr. P. and declares, " that the old Celtic tongue was the mother of the Greek, Latin, Engliſh, Gauliſh and Britiſh ; and it is well known that the Greek and Latin are dead, and the Celᵗic ſurvived them, and will remain in the mountains when Mr. P. is dead alſo."

This man is very inconſiſtent ; for one while he allows that the Cumerag Celtic is ſpoken, and here he makes it quite different from Welſh, or even Iriſh, totally corrupted; though he knows nothing of the matter, but impudently affirms it, as if well verſant, by way of take-in, that the ſuperficial reader may look on him as a man of learning, though the more ſenſible one ſhould judge very differently. If one was diſpoſed to banter and laugh at this gentleman's au miracle au miracle, and his blind dependence on his Welſh and Iriſh intelligence on a language he is not a competent judge of,

here

here is abundance of matter for that kind of paſtime; but the Author has neither time nor inclination to employ his vein of humour ſo triflingly, and affirms *(brevi manu)* that the above raillery is below contempt, and a ſtrong proof that railing with this man muſt be always poured forth, for want of reaſon, to miſlead his reader.

When his argument is plauſible, a convincing return will be always given to ſatisfy the reader, otherwiſe none but ‘ his ‘ *argumentum ad hominem* follows, in tell- ‘ ing that the Dalreads & Tua de Dannan ‘ firſt ſettled in Arguileſhire. In the year ‘ 258, the Scots and Attacotti were driven to ‘ Ireland; yet, on their return in the year 503, ‘ they retained the ſame language they for- ‘ merly had.’

One would imagine that he means the Celtic, if ſuch people as the Dalreads and Tua de Dannan made good their ſettle- ment in Scotland, which by the by is not believed generally; nor is it at all certain or very probable, except by Mr. P. and his Iriſh lucubrations. But paſſing this, he he tells us afterwards, it muſt have been ſome other language.

The Rev. Mr. Whitacre, in his Hiſtory of Mancheſter*, and Genuine Hiſtory of the Britons, has aſſerted that the Scots are deſcended of the Iriſh; yet he muſt acknowledge that in the time of Ammianus Marcellinus, A. D. 340, the Scots were already ſettled in Scotland, or Caledonia; he found them alſo, in 343, concluding a peace with Conſtans, and broke it in his brother's reign; and A. D. 360, he found them alſo in the ſame country. This not only proves their being natives, but their great power long before the year 503, when the Iriſh Scots are fooliſhly ſaid to arrive with the Tua de Dannan and Dalreads, and whoſe numbers were ſo few, according to Mr. Baxter, as hardly to be known until the 7th century, as obſerved alſo by Ravenant the monk, *eeeo obſcuri nominis ut jam ſeptimo exeunte ſeculo, aut ignoti fuerant aut neglecti.* Surely theſe were not the brave people that almoſt conquered the powerful PECHS themſelves, to extend their

territories,

territories, which they might have probably accomplifhed, had not the Picks called in the aid of their Southern neighbours, anno 357, i. e. the Britons, and Romans, to help them to expell thefe Scots from Scotland altogether:—And Fergus II. was only fuffered to return anno 404.

Befides, Roman authors do not afford any hints of the Scotch emigrations from any other country; and an able hiftorian remarks on this head, that all fuch emigrations which have been afferted, or received by Irifh bards, Scotch hiftorians, or Englifh antiquaries, (Buchanan, Cambden, Ufher, Stillingfleet, &c.) are totally fabulous; that three of the Irifh tribes, which are mentioned by Ptolemy, A. D. 150, were of Caledonian extraction; that a younger branch of Caledonian princes of the houfe of Fingal acquired poffeffion of the monaftery of Ireland. Even Whitaker makes thefe conceffions, though a friend to the Irifh romantic extraction of the Scots from the Irifh, and following Richard of Cirencefter,

cefter, a credulous author of the 14th century.

Dr. Macpherfon, fpeaking of the fubject, obferves, that though it has been the general opinion of many nations, that the Scots of Britain have derived their origin from the Irifh ; yet, as the bare authority of a thoufand learned men is not equal to the force of one folid argument, nor the belief of feveral great nations more, in many inftances, than a popular error, it is far from being impoffible that thefe writers and whole nations may have been miftaken in the prefent cafe. That they were actually fo, it is no crime to fufpect, nor an unpardonable prefumption to affirm, when it can be evinced that their belief is ill founded. Upon the whole, we may firmly believe that the native Scots Highlanders had too little room for themfelves in Arguilefhire, and would not fuffer ftrangers from Ireland to creep into the beft part of the country, in fuch circumftances.

So then it is a truth beyond doubt, accord-

ing

ing to hiftory, that, in the year 357, the
Scots were very powerful, infomuch that
the Picts found it neceffary to call the Britons and Romans to their aid, as above,
when they fought on that year a battle
which proved ruinous to the Scots, feeing
the enemy cleared them out of Scotland ;
and were permitted to return from their ba-
nifhment only under the conduct of Fergus II. who was the fecond founder of the
Scotch kingdom, anno 404. Thefe Scots
were very powerful long before the Irifh
Scots were mentioned, and too numerous
to afford room for, or even fuffer ftrangers
to neft among them in the beft part of their
country. It is therefore abfurd to maintain,
that there were no Scots in N. Britain before
504, when the Tua de Dannan & Dalreads,
an imaginary people, are faid to have appeared on the coafts. It is truly affecting
to read of the diftrefs of the Scots before
they yielded to the fuperiority of three
powers ; when their king fays, *Quod potui
feci, quis tantis hoftibus obftet?* And as John-
ffon of Aberdeen writes, *Conjurata acies,
Picti,*

Picti, Britto, Itala Virtus; all the three powers were combined againſt them, before they were beat or baniſhed, in which forlorn ſtate they remained about forty-ſeven years before they were recalled.

There are ſeveral other ancient writers, as well as Ammianus Marcellinus, of opinion, that the Scots began to make a conſiderable figure in the reign of Severus in Scotland. Antoninus Caracalla, the ſon of Severus, put an end to the war in that early period, by receiving hoſtages from the Caledonians and Scots, as remarked by Herodian.

It is certain that only a part of N. Britain was called Scotland; and the name Scot was not appropriated to the whole nation till after Kenneth II. had, about the year of Chriſt 834, ſubdued the Piⅽts, and incorporated them into one nation with our anceſtors. Says Abercromby, " Ireland was called Scotland, and Scotland oftener called Ireland, Ierne."

Sir James Ware, though an Iriſhman, honeſtly confeſſes, that in the Iriſh hiſtories there is much falſehood. That it is probable the Iriſh had their origin
from

from Britain, both by reafon of the vicinity
of Britain, and the eafinefs of the paffage,
as alfo from the conformity of the language
and cuftoms with thofe of the ancient Britons; and if fo, for thefe very reafons, that
part of Britain which lies neareft to Ireland,
whofe language they fpoke, and whofe cuftoms they followed, muft have been their
mother country; for, adds Dr. Mackenzie,
though they would not venture from South
Britain, on fo broad a paffage, there is no
reafon why colonies might not pafs over
from the North even in their little currachs,
to the enjoyment of lands that lay in their
view, either from Cantyre, Arran, Iflay, or
Portpatrick, where the paffage is only
twenty miles over.

It is acknowledged that moft antiquaries
affert that the Scots came from Ireland; but
their opinions are vague and uncertain, as
Dr. Abercromby remarks that fome declare
the Irifh came from Spain, and thefe again
partly from Greece and Egypt; but modern authors, foreigners efpecially, are for
the moft part of opinion that the Scots are

nearer

nearer a-kin to their now neighbours, the Englifh, French, and Spaniards. Dr. George Mackenzie believes that the Scots came originally from Scythia to Norway, from Norway to Scotland, and alfo that the Scots in Ireland went from North Britain.

Bede places the Scots juftly among the old inhabitants of the Ifles. It is plain, according to him, that the Scots had a being in Scotland before the time of Julius Cæfar. Nay, Galcacus, than whom no Pagan Prince made ever a more fhining figure in the Roman Hiftory, fought at the head of the Scots and Picts againft Agricola at the foot of the Grampians, near Angus and Mearns; though at laft the Scottifh fiercenefs gave way to Roman difcipline, and that not long after the Chriftian æra; fo that Bede might with propriety call them ancient refidenters in Scotland—or, in his own words, *prifci incolæ*. Caxton, in his Old Chronicle of England, writes, that the king of the Scots affifted Caffibelan king of the Britons, againft Julius Cæfar, long before the Chriftian æra. In fhort, Baleus, who

is

is much admired by many, is fo juft as to acknowledge that the Scots wrote *ex incorrupta annalium fide*, i. e. faithfully from uncorrupted annals. Among fo many different opinions, is it not fafeft to rely upon the language that fixed the name of thefe people from their profeffi onas failors? even from the word *fcode*, which then, as it does now, fignified a fail, as the failors in Englifh are named from the fame occupation, and which, among the iflanders, was of much older ftanding; though the Romans never heard of it till a much later period, all of which circumftances place them in Scotland long before the Irifh Scots are foolifhly faid to arrive in the South corner of Argyle—and that long after the Scots were banifhed the kingdom, and the return of Fergus the Second, who collected home that fcattered nation again. In one word, the Scots will finally appear, on mature confideration, to be neither more nor lefs than the offspring of the Picts or Caledonians.

'For, fays Mr. P. the Norwegians fettled in

D ·   the

' the Hebrides, in the ninth century, for 400
' years. (He means only a part of that time,
' and that the Isles were not conquered, but
' given up voluntarily we suppose.) And it
' is perfectly known, that the present Gaelic
' of the Highlanders of Scotland is quite full
' of Norwegian words. (By whom is all this
' known so well? That is a secret that must be
' concealed carefully by Mr. Pinkerton from
' the penetrating readers.) Hence, this speech
' is much more corrupt than any other Celtic
' dialect, in as much as its written monu-
' ments are five centuries more modern : for
' in the Islands of the Hebrides, the Celtic
' tongue had a much better chance than in
' the Highlands of Scotland, where constant
' intercourse with the Lowlanders or Picts
' on the one hand, and the Norwegians on
' the other, must have totally changed it.'

Not so bad it is to be hoped, seeing no
violence extraordinary was ever offered to
do so much mischief to it ; no—even if some
kind of force had been used, which was
never the case, to bring about such a revolution. Though some conquests may alter a
· language,

language, yet many do not. Indeed, fays
Mr. Webb, when an invader conquers a
country, and carries off the old inhabitants,
then his own people eftablifhes his own
country language, as the Ifraelites did in Ca--
naan, after expelling the old inhabitants;
and the Jews that were carried to Babylon
loft their own, and adopted the language of
the neighbouring nations; fo that they did
not even know their own language, but
by an interpreter. *

On the contrary, when a conqueror mixes
with the natives; if fmaller in number, then
they adopt the language of the natives; if
equal, it becomes a mixture of languages.
Thus the Lombards brought a new language
into Italy; and the Saracens and Moors
brought a new language into Spain. And
when an invader conquers a country with a
view to exact tribute in token of their fubjection, and immediately quitteth it again,
the language remains as formerly unchange-
able. Thus Alexander the Great never
eftablifhed his own tongue in the kingdom
of Porus, becaufe he only leapt in, and im-

* Neh. cap. 8.

medi-

mediately departed. Neither did the conqueſt of the French in Italy, alter the language of Italy--no more than the invaſions of the Romans and Danes in Scotland made any change in the Celtic or the Gaelic, the language of the country, particularly of the Scots and Piƈts. Sometimes the conquerors are allured to copy the manners and language of the conquered, as the Greeks did of the Perſian luxury, and Romans of the Grecians, particularly of its language, as Plutarch in the Life of Cato writes, that moſt of the Romans ſtudied their Belles Lettres.

Now the Iſles were not conquered, but given up by Donald Bane to the Goths, and that on condition that the natives ſhould neither be removed nor much diſturbed, but be at liberty to keep poſſeſſion of their lands and properties as before under the Kings of Scotland, and only pay tribute to the King of Norway, and acknowledge him as their lawful King in room of the other. Hence are the reaſons why the the Gaelic is not in the leaſt adulterated over all the Uiſts and Barray; and the continual

feuds

feuds kept alive by the natives and foreigners, preferved the language more free from
mixture, or corruption, as Pinkerton calls
it.

" It fometimes happens," fays Dr. Johnfon, " that, by conqueft, intermixture, or
gradual refinement, the cultivated parts of
a country change their language. The moun-
taineers then become a diftinct people, cut
off by diffimilitude of fpeech from converfation with their neighbours. Thus in
Bifcay the original Cantabrian, and in Dale-
carlia the old Swedifh, ftill fubfifts. Thus
Wales and the Highlands of Scotland fpeak
the tongue of the firft inhabitants (Ah!
where is Mr. Pinkerton's changeable language) of Britain, while the other parts
have received the Englifh. That primitive
manners are continued where a native language is fpoken in a nation, no one will
defire me to fuppofe ; for," adds he, " the
manners of the mountains are commonly
favage ; but they are produced rather by
their fituation, than derived from their anceftors."

He further remarks, that the Gothic fwarms

bore

bore no proportion to the inhabitants in whofe country they fettled. This is plain from the paucity of Northern words (this is too much for Mr. P. to bear patiently) now found in the provincial languages, and in the fame proportion thofe Goths in the Hebrides were in comparifon to the multiplicity of the natives. Thefe Norwegian words made no impreffion on the language of the inhabitants, as is too well known to be debated with feeming advantage by any gentleman, though difpofed to be of a contrary opinion.

Mr. Pinkerton's tautology is difgufting, and is alfo moft unlucky in going, like the fhoemaker, beyond his laft; in regard we fee that the very reverfe to the principle he wifhes to eftablifh, is the cafe relative to the Ifles and Scotland. As the Romans could not fix their own language in Britain, fo neither could the Norwegians in the Hebrides; for, except in a few names of ifles, landing places, forts, and little bays or towns, not one veftige of their language remains, or is fpoken even there, where the proprietors were Norwegians, and fome of them ftill continue fo,

The

The natives, who have the advantage of trading with the Danes, and of frequently boarding their veſſels, are after all free from the dialect : and the Author is bold to ſay, with all their ignorance, that they know as much of the language as Mr. Pinkerton does, notwithſtanding his pompous parade of words and vocables produced to convince the ignorant of his extenſive knowledge of that language. For one who ſpent near nine years of his time in theſe very iſles is entitled to know the firſt, and Mr. Pinkerton's groſs miſapplication of vocables encourages him to affirm the laſt.

In Scotland, on the Eaſt ſide in particular, the Gaelic is on the decline, and on the coaſt ſide moſtly forgot, ariſing from a different cauſe, and not from their intercourſe with the Norwegians. But as he affirms that no fragment is older than the fourteenth century, and maintains, with Dr. Johnſon, that no evidence, for a hundred lines, is older written than a century back; ſo it makes one ſuſpect that he was one of thoſe who miſled that learned man, ſeeing he himſelf acknowledges that he ſpoke from information.

D 4   We

We muft then refer Mr. Pinkerton to the Rev. Mr. Mac Nicol, who has trounfed the old man very foundly; and he will convince him, that Gaelic was well known in Scotland long prior to this foolifh date. There is an old woman of my acquaintance in Herries, aged upwards of a hundred years, and fpeaks only the Gaelic taught her by her mother, who alfo was aged before her death; and this woman, ftill alive, remembered her grandmother, and her old faying, which fhe rehearfes to the youngfters in the family by way of advice. Surely the grandmother was cotemporary with King James the Sixth of Scotland, more than two hundred years back; of courfe Mr. Pinkerton's affertion muft fall to the ground. This clergyman, however, will teach him more than reading the thoufands of volumes he announces to the public as a neceffary qualification before any perfon fhould venture to lay his works before their bar for their judgment.

Then we fhall inform him from Mr. Mac Nicol's knowledge, or, if he pleafes, from the Author's own reading, that, anno 1249, a High-

a Highland bard, at the coronation of Alexander the Third, pronounced an oration on
the Genealogies of Kings, prior to the deftruction of any of the records by Edward
the Firſt of England. The bard behoved
to be well verſed in his account before ſo
many learned judges, who could have cor-
rected him had he erred in his narration.

In King James the Sixth's time, two phy-
ficians of the name of Bethune were edu-
cated in Spain ; and one of them, who was
phyfician to the King, wrote a learned treatiſe
on Phyfic, in Gaelic characters. Both of
them were well verſed in Greek and Latin,
and took quotations from Hippocrates ; yet
did not underſtand a word of Englifh. The
one was named Olla Illach, the other Olla
Mulich, from the two Ifles where they
lived—(Olla fignifies a Doctor). All their
pleadings in Courts of Juſtice were in Gaelic;
and there is undoubted teſtimony, even as
late as the old Parliament held at Ard Chattan in Arguilefhire, in Robert Bruce's time,
that Gaelic was the language of their de-
bates; of courſe it could not be an adulterated

rated language, much lefs alterable, when known now, as well as then.

Mr. Innes mentions an old chronicle from Kenneth Mac Alpin's time to Kenneth the Third, the fon of Malcolm, before the year 1291, that was evidently wrote in Gaelic.—And he moreover adds, that Gaelic was fpoken in Galloway in his own time.*

It is to be wifhed that Mr. Pinkerton may preferve his gravity on finding his friend Innes fupporting the old Gaelic of his country: but what fhall he fay, when told that the aged bard's wifh, and *cochag na flrone*, or night owl, go as far back as the ages of hunting, as they contain not the fmalleft veftige of hufbandry, or allufion to agriculture, or any of the modern arts of life, can be produced on it?

Thefe Scots or Caledonians in Galloway remained longer unfubdued by the Scotch Kings than any other people among the fubjeds of the Kings of the Pids; being diffatisfied with the late overthrow, they retired into the remote corners in the South of Scotland.

* 1727.

Andrew,

Andrew, Lifhop of Rofs, fpeaks of a hiftory wrote by a cotemporary writer, under
the title of *Chronicus Antiquorum in Geſtis
& Annalibus Antiquis Scotorum Brittonum.*
This is ſtill extant, and he mentions alſo
the annals of the Piɛts and Scots, and thefe
of fo long a date, that they were efteemed
old then, that is ancient, by an author who
died before the year 1185.* ,

Nay, St. Gildas was born in Scotland, at
Dumbarton, and Gaelic was his mother
tongue. Cumineus, and Adamanus, both
abbots of Iona, wrote, befides the Hiftory
of St. Columbus, other Hiftorical Treatifes;
and we know that thefe flouriſhed 1100
years ago, and they wrote in Gaelic, †
The above will be too much for Mr. Pinkerton to bear with patience; but there is
no help for it. We ſhall hear a little more
of his own account, no lefs difagreeable to
the ear of the fenfible reader, than Innes's
remarks in favour of the Gaelic, are to himfelf.

‘ The Celts being natural favages, and
regarded as fuch by all writers of all ages,

* Innes's Critical Eſſay, &c.   † Ibid.

‘ their

' their tongue was fo fimple whence they
' borrowed of all others ; our Celtic etymo-
' logifts, ignorant of thefe facts, derive many
' words from Celtic, without fufpecting the
' real truth, that the Celtic words are de-
' rived from them. Without a complete
' acquaintance with the Gothic dialect, no
' one ought to meddle with the Celtic ety-
' mology, elfe he will blunder in utter dark-
' nefs,'

And, *pari paffu*, one would as naturally
think that the man who paffes judgment fo
roundly on the Celtic, ought to be better acquainted with it than Mr. Pinkerton, who
is grofsly ignorant of what he condemns
fo unmercifully, being literally ignorant of
the very meaning of the word Celt, as well
as moft other writers, as will appear on fome
future occafion; *quæ culpare foles, ea tu ne
feceris ipfe*; befides the account is unnecef-
fary, as to the Celtic, feeing the Gothic bears
no fimilarity to it either in found or fenfe.
And Mr. John Tolland, in his collection of
feveral pieces, obferves, that without a thorough knowledge of the Celtic language and
books, the Gaclic antiquities can never be

fet

fet in any tolerable light with regard either to words or things, and that many words in Greek and Latin are illuſtrated by it. This laſt remark adds an additional ſplendour to the ſo long deſpiſed Gaelic.

Mr. Thomas Innes candidly enough confeſſes, that his ignorance of the Celtic language diſqualifies him from being a proper judge of its antiquities. ' That being a ' taſk,' ſays he, ' to which I muſt acknow- ' ledge myſelf very unequal, and which ' none but the natives, thoſe of them *who* ' *are learned and ſkilled in their ancient lan-* ' *guage, (with the help of what is more au-* ' *thentic in their hiſtory,)* could, with any ' hopes of ſucceſs, undertake.' And yet Mr. Pinkerton, with all his ignorance, is bold enough to decide on the merits of this tongue, though truly as inſufficient, but more impudent than Mr. Innes was.

' But, ſays Mr. P. the Celtic is a ſavage lan- ' guage, or mixture of many others, ſo ſoft ' and undetermined in orthography, that, as ' Buchanan ſays of the etymology of his time, ' *ex quo libet quod libet fit*, you may make ' what you pleaſe of what you pleaſe.'

That

That gentleman did not fpeak of the Celtic, but fuch languages as he himfelf knew ; and had too much fenfe to fpeak of a language of which he had but an imperfect knowledge ; and of courfe it is great pre-fumption to make ufe of fo high an autho-rity to fupport an opinion fo injurious to a tongue fo truly expreffive as the Gaelic. ' Perhaps,' fays Mr. Smith, ' there never ' was a language better adapted to poetry ' than the Gaelic, as almoft all its words are ' energetical and defcriptive of the objects ' they reprefent, and are alfo, for the moft ' part, an echo to the fenfe.' Harfh ob-jects are denoted by harfh founds, in which confonants greatly predominate ; whilft foft and tender objects and paffions are expreffed by words which bear fome analogy to them in found. The Gaelic language confifts, for the greateft part, of vowels ; hence, in the hands of a fkilful poet, the found varies perpetually with the fubject of difcourfe, and affumes the tone of whatever paffion he is at the time infpired with ; and any perfon acquainted with the Gaelic, will acknow-ledge the juftnefs of Mr. Smith's remark.

Let

Let us now hear Mr. M'Nicol, a perfect
judge of it, as his opinion may alfo be depended upon. ' I have,' fays he, ' a flight
' acquaintance, at leaft, of fome ancient lan-
' guages; I underftand a few living tongues,
' and I can aver, for truth, before the
' world, that the Gaelic is as copious as
' the Greek, and not lefs fuited to poetry
' than the modern Italian.' Things of
foreign and of late invention may not probably have obtained names in Gaelic; but
every object of nature, and every inftrument
of common and general ufe, has many vocables to exprefs it, fuch as fuit all the various changes that either the poet or orator
may choofe. To prove the copioufnefs of
our language, it is fufficient to affure the
public, that we have a poetical dialect, as
well as one fuitable to profe only; that the
one never encroaches on the other, and that
both are perfectly underftood by the moft
illiterate Highlander.

The chief defect in our language proceeds
from what is reckoned the greateft beauty
in other languages; it has too many vowels
and diphthongs, which, though fuitable to

poetry, renders the pronunciation lefs diftinct and marked, than happens in lefs har-
monious, and confequently, more barbarous
tongues. Some ignorant writers of the
Gaelic of late, it is true, briftled over
their compofitions with too many confonants ; but they are generally quiefcent in
the beginning and end of words, and are
preferved only to mark the etymon.

' Yet ftill,' adds P. ' every name that is
' thought to fpring from the Celtic, may,
' with equal propriety, be applied to others;
' and I fhall engage to derive them with
' equal fitnefs, from any tongue in the world,
' with the help of a dictionary.' Fairly ventured, let us hear him !—' Suppofe,' (continues he) ' we fhould take the Spanifh *fonada-*
' *chanca & ardid* for a fpecimen, and apply
' them to names in the Highlands, Arguile-
' fhire ; take *fonachan & ardinali* for inftance,
' which ftart firft to my eye, *viz. fonada* a
' tune, and *chanca* a jeft ; *(fonadachanca,)* a
' place where they ufed to fing and play ;
' *ardid*, a ftratagem, and *mal, ill*, where a
' confpiracy againft Fingal was defeated.'

7   Where

When it fuits his purpofe, he allows Fingal to have had an exiftence; in other refpeɛts, no fuch perfon lived, and the ftory of that hero is a falfehood of Macpherfon's fabrication.

Here, however, this ambidextrous gentleman has failed in the very firft trial of his fkill, becaufe both the found and fenfe difagree with thefe names in Gaelic; for the fignification of his firft Italian word, which fignifies a place for finging and dancing, is not more adapted to that agreeable piece of entertainment, than to all other parts over the North-weft Highlands, mufick and dancing being a great part of their paftime : but the real Englifh is, a fortunate field; *ach*, a field, and *fonn* lucky or fortunate. He is equally unhappy in *aird mali*, for a plain field ; *aird* is high, and *mali* the fummit or face of that apex, and there is a *dall mhali* at the bottom of that eminence, where a parifh church ftands.

A C H

' Is a river in the old German language, ' and he applies this exotic ach to Auchter- ' tool, Auchinfleet, and Auchinleck.' This may be true with regard to the German ach ;

but ach in the Gaelic is invariably applied to a plain cultivated field, and never once to a river, as his Germans do.—Who knows but Mr. Pinkerton will be more happy in his choice of Gothic words? Let us try his

‘ ARAN,

‘ the name of a man, in Torfæi, *Aroe* an ifle ‘ in the Baltic.’

But *Aran* in the Weft of Scotland derives the name from *Iar* weft, and *Inn*, or *Innifh*, an ifland, *Iarinn* ; or, from bread, *Aran* in Gaelic, the ifle being fertile in corn : it however takes its name from the firft of the two.

‘ MULL,

‘ From Mol, a found in Norway.’ But, on the contrary, that in Scotland has the name from a bank of fand or gravel collected by the fea billows, and is dry at ebb, where people may land from their boats. And the whole ifle takes the name from a part, as Scotland is foolifhly faid to have derived its name from the few men of that appellation, who landed from Ireland in the fouth corner of Argylefhire, *(pars pro toto)*.

‘ HARRIS,

' HARRIS,

' From Haar, high ; or Heroe, an ifle in
' the (Baltic) coaft of Norway.' But *Heuruibh*, a hill, gave the epithet to Harris ;
and that country in Gaelic is always termed
Heuruibh, by all the people in Scotland who
underftand that tongue.

' LIEWIS,

' From the Lees, or loweft part.' But
this had its name from *Sorrachadh*, Sarah, a
woman's name, and is ftill a common chriftian one there, perhaps as old as Abraham's
time, whofe wife bore that name ; that was
originally the appellation given to the Long
Ifle in Scotland. It is known now by the
word Leofe.

' SKIA,

' Corruptedly called Skye, from Skua, one
' of the Ferroe ifles.' But that ifle in the
weft of Scotland derived the name from
SKIA a fhield, SKIAN a dirk or a fword,
and NEACH a people, *i. e.* SKIAN-NEACH;
thefe arms making up part of the drefs of the
inhabitants of this ifle in hoftile times,
when arms and war were the daily employ-
ments of thefe warlike people, and fo might

E 2   well

well be called SKIAN and NEACH—the people with the dirks or fwords, fkian-neach—
and by no means from the Alatis of Buchanan
and others, who called it the Winged Ifle, on
account of the many inlets of fea-lochs—for
every other ifle or coaft-fide is equally fubject
to thefe with Skye, though no people were
more formidably accoutred with arms than
the SKIAN-NEACH were; becaufe they had
not only their own feuds, but alfo the inhabitants of the Long Ifle, ftretching along
on the Weft, North Weft fide, and of Scotland on the Eaft, to guard againft, who
were ready to break in upon their rich ifle
from every quarter to plunder it—And Mr.
Pinkerton does not explain his Skua to form
an opinion of it properly.

‘ DEE

‘ Is a Cumerag name, from water, and
is Welch.’   Mr. Pinkerton may reftore it
back to the Welch when he pleafes, as there
is no river of that name in Gaelic;—but
Diann, a river at Aberdeen, from the fwift-
nefs or rapidity of the ftream—and another,
Donn, from deep, a heavy running river
within a mile of the *Diann* in North Britain.

‘ SUTHER-

' SUTHERLAND

' Is Gothic, becaufe the Goths lived in
' the Orkneys.' But Sutherland is not
in the Orkneys, neither does it derive that
name from the Goths, as fhall appear more
fully elfewhere—nor was it the original—
and but lately the prefent Gaelic name of
that country: but *Gallibh* and *Cattibh* or
Cattee; in Englifh, Caithnefs and Sutherland:
—this laft derives the name from the excellent Spearmen, *i. e. Saor Lannich* or Eaft
Lannies of Strathern (or Stirlingfhire)of old.

' TAY

' Is by all appearance Gothic; Tavus,
' Tau, Au, or Aa, is a river in Germany.' It
is acknowledged that *Tamh*, is the deep fea,
or main ocean in Gaelic, and the flow deep
running river from *Loch Tamh*. Tay may
derive its name from that fource without
feeking after it in Germany.

FORTH is perfect Gothic, *Fiorda*, a Firth.
This is granted him, for Forth is not Gaelic;
he may referve it for the Gothic Piks, when
they arrive. But this betrays Mr. Pinkerton's ignorance. For *Bodotria* is the name
given to that river by Tacitus, and the fol-

E 3   lowers

lowers of the Romans, from *bod* a boat, and *otter* a collection of mud and dirt caſt into a ſoft heap, either by the ſea or rivers, into any quiet corner of a loch, bay, or river, over which no boat can paſs, nor man walk upon at ebb ſea or low water. And the bottom of the Forth is perfectly impaſſable either for horſe or footmen, in moſt parts of it, owing to the deep clay channel of 50 odd miles through which that water runs; and when it overflows its banks, there is hardly getting to a boat through the mud and dirt left behind it.—So much for the Forth.

But indeed Tacitus writes about this Bodotria in ſuch dubious terms, ariſing, both from his ignorance of the country, and want of accurate information of the true name of that famous river; that one is at a loſs to know whether he means not Clyde as much as the Forth, from the narrow iſthmus that almoſt joins the two. For though he writes that, in the fourth ſummer of Agricola's command, *Glotta & Bodotria diverſi maris æſtu per immenſum revecti anguſto terrarum ſpatio dirimuntur, quod tum præſidiis firmaba-*

tur,

*tur, atque omnis propior finus tenebatur, fum-
motis velut in aliam,* &c. the Bodotria and
Glotta being feparated by a peninfula;
yet on the third fummer, he writes that
he met with new nations: *Novas gentes
aperuit vaftatis ufque ad T aum,* &c. which he
laid wafte as far as the Tay river *(Æftuario
nomen eft) nationibus* &c. and what is furprifing,
it is only in the fixth fummer that we find
him oppofed by the Caledonians: *Ceterum
æftate qua fextum officii annum inchoabat, amplas civitates trans Bodotriam fitas,&c.—Infefta
hoftili exercitu itinera timebantur, prius claffe
exploravit, &c.—Ad manus ad arma converfi
Caledoniam incolentes populi, &c.—Fuit atrox
in ipfis portarum anguftiis prælium, donec pulfi
hoftes utroque exercitu, his ut tuliffe opem; illis
ne eguiffe auxilium viderentur, quid nifi paludes
& filvæ fugientes texiffent debellatum illa victo-
ria foret.* But though the barbarians were
worfted in this hot engagement, they were
not difheartened, as might well be expected
from the bold unconquered Caledonians, in
fo much that Agricola found it convenient
to go cautioufly to work againft them afterwards, as we may gather from what he re-

E 4   marks

marks of their prudence, caution, and loud boafting: *Atqui illi modo cauti, ac fapientes, prompti poft eventum, ac magniloqui erant* Thus it feems they were far from being difpirited by their late misfortune.

The only difficulty is, to find out the proper place where this engagement happened. Boetius, who follows and agrees with Cambden, draws a wall between the Efk to the mouth of the river Tweed, which, fays he, Tacitus calls it *Taum Æftuarium.* But Sir James Dalrymple affirms, that the learned Cambden has been miftaken, when he fays that Tweed was the fame river which Tacitus called *Taus*, fince it is plain from Tacitus his account that Taus was near the Grampian hills in Perthfhire, whither the Romans, after they had beat the enemy, carried their arms through the country of Perthfhire and Angus, and ordered the fleet to fail about the ifle. Sir George MacKenzie is alfo of this laft opinion.

It is however no unpardonable crime to differ in fentiments with thefe two learned baronets; efpecially when we find the firft engagement with the Romans, the fixth

Summer,

Summer, to have happened on the South fide
of the Forth, *citra Bodotriam*, and that Agricola drew up his forces oppofite to Ireland,
which muft be underftood either to be *Jura,
Arran*, or *Bute* ifles, for he could not mean
the prefent Ireland, becaufe the neareft to
Scotland being 20 miles, too great a diftance
to ftrike terror into the inhabitants of it,
while the other ifles were within view of
the army drawn up in Airfhire, and the people might juftly be alarmed by fuch a fight.
Yet though the firft fkirmifh happened on
the fixth year, when he drew off his troops,
and croffed Clyde in the firft boat that he
met with, and then paffed into a country unknown before, he fays, *Quinto anno nave
prima tranfgreffa, ignotas ad id tempus gentes
crebris fimul ac profperis præliis domuit*; that
is, after paffing over at *Bad Ottir*, near Dunbarton, or the Clyde, he was then literally
entered among the nations before unknown
to the Romans ; and after fecuring himfelf
from the inhabitants as well as he could, he
might be engaged on the fixth Summer, not
on the fifth, as above, almoft in the very mouth
of the harbour, by the fierce people, who had
collected

collected their forces to prevent his marching through their country.

I am therefore more inclined to join Cambden, than the learned Baronets ; becaufe it is not probable that fo cautious a General as Agricola would venture his forces at firft into the heart of a ftrange country, in the moft dangerous part of all Britain, and fo far removed from any affiftance from his friends in cafe of a defeat, or deftruction of his fleet, by enemies fo terrible as the unconquered Caledonians : he being about 80 miles in that cafe from the provinces, and on the North of the Forth, with almoft impaffable forefts, mountains, fwamps, and rivers, all within the power of the enemy, who would throw every block in his way, and even remove their boats from the Forth, to render their paffage over that large river impracticable, and almoft impoffible, in cafe of misfortune ; a thing naturally to be expected when encountering the high-fpirited Caledonians. Whereas his landing his troops at the Tweed, or rather farther up the Forth, though he fhould meet the enemy, as we find he did, and even

be

3

be worſted by them ; yet he was in Valentia, where the Romans had friends, and where he might recover himſelf without running the riſque of total deſtruction ; as his landing at the Firth of Tay, between Angus and Fife, might be attended with.

Beſides his advancing up to the iſthmus near Stirling, along the river Forth, while he was ſafe, he was alſo as near the Grampians, much nearer Air, to frighten the iſlanders, and in fact at the mouth of the Taichica Vallis, or Monteith, called in Gaelic *Stra Tauich*, where the rivers Teith and Forth join, and gave a name to the whole valley on the ſides of the Forth ;· whereas the Strath above the Tay is called Strathern, Vallis Ernica, a name well known now, as well as then. Had the above Baronets known this, they certainly would not imagine that the General would act ſo inadvertently, and even fooliſhly, by landing ſo far North, then marching his troops 100 miles to the South, to Airſhire, and the year after return back to Strathern to fight with Galcacus about Stonehive in Angus ſhire.

No,

No, furely; he certainly landed on the South of the Forth, and gradually marched Northward by Camelodunum, and Stirling, or Alloa; thefe large cities, as Tacitus writes :—then to Ardoch, where he made a camp ; and afterwards to Strathern, where he made another on the plains of *Dealgen-rofs*; and from thence towards the Eaft Sea, where he might meet his fleet, on board of which he placed his forces, after fighting with Galcacus at the foot of the Grampians. —But we fhall return back after this digref-fion, to enquire into the true name of the Forth.

And the real name of that river was, and is ftill, in Gaelic, POULL, UISG A PHUILL and derives its name from the fource ; it dif-charges its waters into another river at *Ab-berfoil*, a parifh in Perthfhire well known by that name. And feveral gentlemen's feats receive their names from it; from the fource almoft to Edinburgh.

About 14 miles below the above parifh ftands Wefter Poull Aird ; four miles farther down, we meet with Eafter Poull Aird ; below

low this, one meets with a Mid Poull Aird. This (*Aird*) fignifies a houfe of entertainment or hofpitality for paffengers, in cafe they were late, or prevented from paffing the ferry by times. — About four miles weft of Stirling, befide the river Poull, lies *Loch Taobh Phuill*, called Lochtafill. — There are twenty-four miles of water between the caftle of Stirling and the town of Alloa, a fpace of four miles only by land. The meanders or links of the river Forth prefent the eye with the moft beautiful landfcape on earth from that caftle. Among the gentle heavy windings and turnings of that large river, *Fallihn*, or *Poull Linnidh*, a deep lake, and Cook's Pows, or Poull, are two famous places well known to have derived their names from the river *Poull*; and below Falkirk, another gentleman's feat of the name of Bruce ftands, and called Bofoulls, or in Gaelic, *Bo* a town, and *Poull* the river; all thefe on the bank mark the name of the river, and are facts that cannot be controverted, at leaft overturned by Mr. Pinkerton.

Boetius

Boetius remarks, that the more pure and genuine reading is found in an old copy of Tacitus. *Ampla civitas trans Badotriam fita:* this is the literal Gaelic, free from corruption, *Bad-ottir*; and very probably Camelodunum on the South of the Forth was the city alluded to, for the Romans had not then croſſed over the river Forth, or Poull. Therefore Stillingfleet calls Clyde the Otter, which is more probable, becauſe there is a ferry-boat by Dunbarton called Otter Ferry or Bad Otter, over which Agricola with his Romans paſſed, after he had drawn off his army from the coaſt of Air, where they were drawn up as if to terrify the people of Ireland with an invaſion, or rather the little Iſle of Arran or Iſla, (for it is impoſſible as above he would mean to frighten the inhabitants of the preſent Ireland, an iſland at a diſtance of more than 20 miles from the neareſt part of Scotland, from whence the eye could not ſee a man nor an army): and by this ferry-boat there ſtands a hill called *Dun-Ottir* a little way from the caſtle of Dunbarton. There is another *Bad-Ottir* about three miles

from

from the mouth of Loch-finn, in Cowal, with many more that might be fpecified, had not thefe been fufficient to convince Mr. Pinkerton, that the name in every point of view has been mifunderſtood and mifapplied by others as well as by himfelf; fo that here he has erred in good company, fo much for his comfort!

‘ GRAMPIANUS,

‘ Surely from Gram, a town in Norway.’ Worfe and worfe !—for inftead of a town, the Grampians of Scotland are hills, *i. e.* *Garabh-Bheantibh*, rugged hills.

OCHILL,

‘ This name is Welch, from High Ochill.’ But thofe in Scotland receive their names from wood, and hill—*uchdan wacher*, always applies to a little hill; *direadh re uchdan*, mounting the hill or eminence. And it is clear that the beautiful Ochil-hills in Scotland were covered over with wood, as is known from the veftiges of it to this day. Wachd-Coill, contracted Ochil, the woody hill; for *caill* is wood, and *uchd* an hill, *uchd-caill*; and there is a town in its vicinity

named

named *Ochterarder*, that is, *wach ar ardan*, a town on the fummit of an eminence or rifing ground in Perthfhire.

' LONDON,

' From *Lond*, a grove, *i. e.* a town in a grove.' Why not the name that was originally given it? as LON and DUN; the firft fignifies a ftore of provifion, and the latter the hill on which the faid ftore was laid out of the boat, either at Tower-hill, or Fleet-ftreet hill; for Ludgate is precifely LOD or FLOD a fleet, and *geott* an inlet of the river; and it is well known that the fleet paffed up to the head of Fleet-market once, though now the *gcott* is covered over with an arch, over which the market ftands.

Edward Llhyd and others are too honeft to arrogate to themfelves names not to be met with in the Welch or Englifh language, and acknowledge thefe names to belong to the original inhabitants, who certainly fpoke Gaelic, as the above names are well known by the inhabitants of North Britain to this day, and many more fuch to be met with over all England and Wales, and totally un-known to the prefent inhabitants.

' ABBIR,

' ABBIR :

' Here follows a world of Abers, as
' Aberfoil, &c. both in Scotland, Germany ;
' and Gothland, (and Mr. P. has exerted
' his ingenuity to make them anſwer other
' purpoſes, than their meaning in GAELIC ;
' laſt of all, he gravely tells his Engliſh
' reader, for it is impoſſible he ſhould ima-
' gine that any judge would believe him,)
' this poor Aber, which has been tortured
' into ſo many meanings, is abſolutely the
' German Ubber, *beyond,* and means a
' town beyond a river.' After ſo decided a
judgement, it would be in vain to tell
this pragmatic gentleman, that in Gaelic
Aber uniformly ſignifies the mouth of a
river where its waters are diſcharged into
the ſea, loch, or ſome other river, and
not once uſed for the prepoſition *beyond.*

' BAL :

' As Balmerino, Balcaras. This is ano-
' ther word that would puzzle the moſt
' profound etymologiſts, ſays he, to deter-
' mine *if really* Celtic or Gothic. Nothing
' is more certain than that the Icelandic,

F   ' or

' or Gothic, is a town or village'. This is granted him—but we fee no reafon for borrowing from the Goths, as the Celtic is fo compleatly fupplied with *Ba*, *Bo*, and *Bal* of their own, as well as of others, without calling in foreign aid from thefe countries.

' DAL

' Seems to be equivalent to *Bal* in Scot-
' land, as Dalrymple,—fo alfo in *Norway*
' and *Denmark.*' But though Mr. P. mif-leads his Englifh reader, I defy him to do fo to a Highlander, who is certain that *Dal* is not once applied to a town, but always to a beautiful plain field at the head or end of a promontary, or angle cut by a river, as DALCAN Ross—Dealgin-rofs in Pertfhire, where a Roman camp is to be feen.

' KIN,

' As *Kinkell*; thefe are not fimilar to names
' in Wales or Ireland, and will of them-
' felves turn this point quite the other way.
' For there are 30 of them in England, and
' only *Kinfale* in all Ireland, as may be feen

' in

' in the Index Valaris. This was the place
' from whence formerly the king failed.' Ay,
where is Kinſburrow, near Cork ? and Kin,
a burrow of Carrig, and another Kin, of
Boyle ? and Kinlis, *i. e.* CEAN LISE,
the head of a garden, or fertile field in
Meath ? This Fickle Index has betrayed
poor P. into a ſnare, and no wonder by
placing ſuch confidence in it, he ſhould
fall into the ditch—as his leader was as
ignorant of this KIN, as he is himſelf.
Wo is me, then, the ſcale is turned upon
himſelf, like a man's head broke by his
own ſtaff, for *Kin* and *ſale* ſignifies the
head, or end of a ſalt water loch, and *Kin-*
kell in Scotland, is the end of a wood,
Cean-coill.

'ERSKIN

' Is the very ſame thing, with Kinſale;' (it
is ſuppoſed ſo,) but it is no ſuch matter
in faƈt; but AR, upon, and SKIAN, a
dirk or knife, the head of a wolf, upon
the point of a dagger, or ſword ; and few
kings ever failed with pleaſure on ſuch
a vehicle ; and all put together expoſes
F 2   Mr.

Mr. P. the more, like the monkey, the higher it climbs, the barer its tail appears, and of courfe the more laughable to the fpectators.

' FORR:

' This word is uncertain; as Fordun.' But in Gaelic it is by no means uncertain, being equivalent to FARIDH, watch, and DUN, a hill, *a watch hill* to fpy the enemy, fomething like the Norwegian *Gok man* on his watch tower. —

' Two thirds of the names of the *Ebudæ* ' Iflands and Highlands, are infallibly Go- ' thic.' Here Mr. P. thought that his going to the remote Ebudæ would infallibly fcreen him from detection; but he happens to be unfortunately miftaken; for the affertion is abfolutely denied, and the author ought to know better than Mr. Pinkerton, or even his Atlas, and Gothic Dictionaries; for he not only was long in the country, knows the language, and was born in Scotland, where the Gothic is unknown, but the GAELIC perfectly familiar to every ear there, where the language

guage is fpoke, and ought, on that account,
to gain more credit than any man who
is a perfect ftranger to it, however im-
pertinently prefumptuous; and Mr. P.'s
placing *Sky* among the 5 Ebudes; an
Ifland 36 miles diftant from thefe Ifles,
which are known to be contiguous to one
another, may fatisfy any difcerning reader,
how much he takes upon him above his
knowledge, or any good authority which
is fufficient to convince people of his grofs
miftake. And further, the author, from
his own knowledge, maintains, in direct
oppofition to Mr. P. that except the fmaller *ifles, forts, bays* and *landing-places*, there
are few, if any Gothic words ufed in common converfation, even among the vulgar,
who could not conceal, nor equivocate, if
any fuch were mixed with their language;
fo that the *Danes*, though they refided
long there, have made no alteration in their
language, or the names of *mountains, rivers,*
ftraiths, valleys, and rocks, with frefh and
falt water *lakes* and *lochs*, which alfo are
moftly Gaelic; and this is affuredly the cafe

F 3   in

in Scotland, and more particularly, when
neither *Danes*, nor *Romans*, nor *English*
would be allowed to keep poffeffion by force
of arms, to adulterate their tongue. Thus
Mr. P's 12000 names in Scotland, of which
he fays 30 only are *Welch*, and not above 50
Irifh, on the *north, fouth, and caft*, with
his 2000 *Gothic* words in the *weft*; may in
a great meafure be laid up in the great Atlas
until the Gothic *Piks* are fully eftablifhed
there to make ufe of them.

We fhall follow him fome farther to be informed that he dwelt on this matter, ' be-
' caufe Celtic etymology is become the fren-
' zy of this fhallow age ; and I fhall remark,
' before quitting it, that by Gothic names,
' I mean, fays he, fuch whofe form is Gothic,
' and may be traced in the northern king-
' doms, *Germany* and *England*;' and he concludes with a hope that he has fatisfactorily
anfwered the whole arguments. Here he
does not tell us whofe arguments he thus
belabours, only it is to be fuppofed he means
thofe of the two Mr. Macpherfons, and
thinks his Englifh readers, becaufe ignorant

of

of the *Celtic*, will reft as much fatisfied, though as little edified, as any old woman is after hearing mafs performed in Latin, and yet fhe feals the fervice with an Amen.

We venture to affirm and predict, unlefs his promifed hiftory of Scotland be worded more cautioufly and fupported by better authority, than his enquiry is, that he will gain few profelytes among readers of tafte and learning, to adopt his principles, even with all the aid that his atlas and lexicons can bring to his affiftance.

And tho' we are heartily fick with following this ftrange medley of impertinent vocables of his; yet the kind indulgence of the reader is folicited, while an attempt is made even without the aid of dictionaries and lexicons to fhow Mr. P. that *Celtic* names might with as great propriety be quoted from the *Chinefe*, *Japanefe*, *Tartars*, the wild inhabitants of *N.* and *S. America*, *Arabia*, or even from the Greeks and Romans, as from the Goths, &c. as we are a little better acquainted with the two laft mentioned, than with any of the others, we

F 4 fhall

ſhall venture to make the trial, by way of experiment between the *Latin* and *Gaelic*, then take the ſame method with the *Greek* ; and after comparing a few vocables with a ſentence from each, it is to be hoped that the ſound and ſenſe, and almoſt the ſpelling, will be more adapted to each other than ei-ther the Gothic or German is to the Celtic.

As we have already remarked that moun-tains, rivers and proper names, are allowed to be the moſt unalterable, we ſhall begin therefore with the

Latin.	Gaelic.	Englijh.
Mens,	Mon,	a mountain.
Montes Albini,	Monti Alabinich,	Albion mountains.
Grampiani Montes,	Garabh Mhonti,	rugged mountains.
Amnis,	Ambuin,	a river.
Tiber,	Tober,	a ſpring well, a deep river or ſource, from whence a river takes the name.
Canes,	Cainn,	dogs.
Equus,	Each,	a horſe.
Gallus,	Cailleach,	a cock.
Taurus,	Taura,	a bull.
Arma,	Airm,	arms.
Vir,	Fer,	a man.
Bos,	Bo,	an ox, or cow.

Hores,

Latin.	Gaelic.	English.
Heres,	*Eire,*	an heir.
Dux,	*Deuc,*	a duke.
Comes,	*Compan,*	a companion.
Princeps,	*Priunsa,*	a prince.
Deus,	*Dia,*	God.

Let us now try a fentence; and this is more than what Mr. P. durft venture on.

LATIN.

Cano virumque arma, ab oris Trojæ.

GAELIC.

Caninim fer cu arma, bho oir Traagh.

ENGLISH.

I fing of the hero, and arms, from the coaft of Troy.

We fhall next try whether Homer, &c. underftood the Celtic.

Greek.	Gaelic.	English.
Μονος Ιδα,	*Mon Idi,*	a hill in Perth- fhire.
Μονος Καυκασυς,	*Mon Chamfay,*	a hill in Stirling- fhire.
Τυραννυς,	*Tighearn,*	a laird, tyrant.
Ηερκυλες,	*Hircle,*	Hercules.
Παρις,	*Parick,*	Peter, a Trojan.
Μενελαος,	*Ma lane,*	M'Millan.

Greek.	Gaelic.	English.
Ηεκτορ,	Eachan,	a Trojan hero.
Πενελοπε,	Penelope,	a woman's name.
Ηελευ,	Ellen,	a woman's name.
Γαλατεα,	Galatea,	a wanton girl.

Hector, advifing the Grecians and Trojans to allow Paris and Menelaus to decide
the controverfy by fingle combat, addreffes
them thus :

Κεκλευτε μευ Τροης, και ευκνημιδες Αχαιοι.
Clunibl ini Thraerin cu oig na min chos'mhie Wyii, i.e. M'K y's.
Hearken to me, Trojans, and ye well-booted, or limb'd
Grecians.

Οκεανος Θαλασσα, nCuan Sallach, or (boif-
terous) ocean.

Was I to look into Dictionaries and Lexicons, perhaps Virgil or Homer might be
introduced fpeaking *Gaelic* in the Æneid
and Iliad ; but from this hafty fpecimen, it
is referred to any judicious reader, nay,
even to Mr. P. himfelf, whether the parallel given has not a more ftriking likenefs
than any of his names ; and had he ventured on a whole fentence of his Gothic
language, to compare it with GAELIC or
English,

Englifh, he certainly would cry out *Pec-cavi*, after expofing the fhocking diffimila-rity, as well in fenfe as in found.

And though the Romans refided in Bri-tain for four centuries, it would be thought impertinent, was an attempt made to con-vince the reader, that either borrowed their whole language from the other, becaufe a few vocables and fentiments are alike in fenfe and found.

Mr. P. ftill goes on in his own humour of railing againft the *Celts*. ' The *Celts* ' being indeed mere favages, and worfe than ' the favages of America, and remarkable ' even to our own time, for a total neglect ' of agriculture themfelves, and for plun-' dering their neighbours.' That this out-rage is no lefs futile than fallacious will be obvious to any perfon who travels either by land or fea along the weft coaft or the ifles of Scotland, where many ftately edi-fices have been raifed by the induftrious inhabitants, both on the coafts as well as in the ifles, where alfo every other fpecies of

improvement,

improvement is carried on with judgment and tafte.

And their great improvements in agriculture are known in London from Dr. Johnfon's account of the improvements he faw in the Ifle of Coll: even in the weftern Ebudæ; one or two of the firft farmers in North Britain refide, Mac Donald of *Boifdale*, whofe polite accomplifhments few can excel, fupports 60 or 70 families on wafte lands, that formerly did not yield ten marks to his father of yearly rent; befides he has much lands inclofed within his own elegant policy, which was equally ufelefs to his father. This gentleman not only raifes the fineft wheat, but makes it into flour in his own mill.

Even Mr. Knox, in his tour, alfo reprobates the foolifh affertions of Mr. P. refpecting the great improvements made every where over the Weft Highlands and Iflands, and writes from his own knowledge, and not from information, which is the moft certain of any. Roots, fays he, vegetables, fallads, and common fruits can be raifed on

the

the weft coafts and iflands of North Britain
in any quantity. Their kail and cabbage
are only exceeded in delicacy by their tur-
nip, which for its flavour, and the finenefs
of its grain is prefented raw at genteel tables, with fruits, wild berries, with fine
dulce, flack, admirably well dreffed by
way of defert. Potatoes are very plenty
through the whole highlands. A fmall
portion of lime, or fhelly fand, where cut,
or caft ware cannot be had for manure,
brings forward a plentiful crop, and of a
quality greatly fuperior to thofe that are
raifed on richer foils.

In the iflands and on the weft coafts of
Scotland, great quantities of kelp are manu-
factured by the induftrious inhabitants, (thefe
are not the indolent favages of Mr. P. furely
not, he muft mark out their lurking places
of abode ;) and the profits arifing from
the kelp made by thefe induftrious people,
are extremely advantageous to the poffeffors
of thefe coafts, whether proprietor or tackf-
men.

And

And fuch of them as anfwer the favage defcription given by Mr. P. fo foully illibe- ral, if he means the better fort, are limited to a very few of that clafs. It is true there are fome thieves of cattle in thefe extenfive countries; but not numerous, nor fo dan- gerous, as in other places, either about large cities in Scotland, and through many parts of England; but few pick-pockets to fteal a purfe, or take a life for it, refide there. That low practice a highlander would fpurn at the thought of: and Mr. P. might travel over hills and dales in the highlands, and fleep in the defarts, or by the way fide there, and he would after he awoke find that his purfe was fafe, and his perfon un- touched by the favages he calls plunderers; this is more than he can tell where he is; nay, nor at Edinburgh, though he refided there. And to brand a whole people for the crimes of a few only is a cruel piece of iniquity in any author. Whoever reads Lanne B.'s travels in the Hebrides, there he will find the moft induftrious commoners

in

in Britain, without exception or difparagement to others, fully defcribed.

 ' Again Mr. P. feizes the two Mr. Mac-
' pherfons by the collars for confidering
' themfelves of the old highland race,
' and opening their mouths like feana-
' chies as they are, and fwallowing up the
' Picts at one mouthful with their hiftory,
' and converted them into *Scots* and *Celts*,
' and alfo denied all the Pictifh hiftory: but
' the grand characteriftic of the *Celts* is to
' put *falfehood* for truth, and truth for *falfe-*
' *hood.* This man was a Doctor of Divi-
' nity, and yet if he had ufed the fame li-
' berty in private bufinefs, which he has
' done in his hiftory, he would have been
' fet in the pillory, and no wonder, though
' he wifhes the deftruction of Innis's hif-
' tory, to make *Offian* and *falfehood* triumph.

In anfwer to this abufe of Mr. P. againft
the Macpherfons and the *Celts,* I muft apply Mr. Mac Nicol's rod of correction to
fcourge him into good manners, as he did
to Johnftone on a fimilar occafion, and leave
with him to confider of his danger. Such

an

an invidious charge as *lying* is the laft thing
that a gentleman fhould be abufed with.
And to bring forward fuch an accufation
without proof to eftablifh it, is a ruffian
mode of impeachment. Doctor Macpherfon was incapable of acting fo bafely, tho'·
Mr. P. is void of candor, and good manners.
The indelicacy of fuch language is obvious ;
a gentleman, fays Mr. Mac Nicol, would
not have expreffed himfelf in that manner
for his own fake ; a man of prudence would
not have done fo for fear of giving juft offence to Mr. Macpherfon. He feems to
have been carelefs about the reputation of
the firft of thefe characters, and the malignity of his difpofition feems to have made
him overlook the forefight generally an-
nexed to the fecond ; though he was bold
in his affertions, he was not equally cou-
rageous in their defence. His mere allega-
tion on a fubject he could not underftand
was unworthy of the notice of the gentleman accufed ; but the language which he
expreffed deferved chaftifement. And men,
who break in upon the laws of good manners,

ners, have but a fcurvy claim to the protection of any other laws. Mr. P. has then
exhibited this fpecimen of his rancour to
no other purpofe, than either to gratify the
prejudiced, or impofe on the weak and credulous.

Saxo Grammaticus, Mr. P.'s great favourite, in direct oppofition, gives a moft
favourable account of the honour of the
Gaels, and their extreme reluctance to fal-
fify, or break their word, and narrates a
melancholy account given of a murder committed in miftake by a tender hufband on
his deareft lady, and the difficulty to which
the King was put to, both to keep his word
and oath, and preferve the life of a mife-
rably unhappy fon-in-law. Nothing, fays
he, but violence makes a King of the Scots
break his oath, for every tye is on him——
*Trahebat itaque regem hinc, in filiam pietas,
in generum amor, inde charitas in ami-
cum, preterea juris jurando firmitas, ipfa
quoque mutuæ obligationis religio, quam
violare nefarium erat.* Thus we find a
fample of real honour between pity to-

G   wards

wards his daughter, and love to his fon-in-
law, from thence charity to his friend, befides the ftrength of an oath, which religion
herfelf defires not to violate, (being an ob-
ligation that is mutual,) and makes a breach
truly nefarious : had Mr. P. known the
better part of thefe people, his rage againft
them would become lefs violent. And mo-
deration arifing from known truths would
have rendered his writings more admired *.

After defcribing the difference between
the highlanders and lowlanders, Mr. P.
adds, ' in mind and manners the diftinction
is marked.'

' The lowlanders are acute, active, in-
' duftrious, free; the highlanders ftupid,
' indolent, flavifh, foolifh, fawning; the
' former in fhort have every attribute of a
' civilized people, the latter are abfolute
' favages, and will continue fo till the race
' be loft by mixture. In vain do we dream
' of building towns in the highlands, if peo-
' pled with highlanders, they will be in
' ruins in lefs than a century. Had all the

* Gaudentius Merula de Gallorum Antiq. 1538.

' Celtic

' Celtic cattle emigrated fome centuries ago,
' how happy had it been for that country.
' All we can do is, to plant colonies among
' them, and by encouraging emigration try
' to get quit of the breed. The *Celts* are
' mere favages, moft tenacious of their
' fpeech and manners. Mr. Macpherfon
' will have it, that Saxon merchants intro-
' duced the Englifh tongue; what a bull !
' no, nor the nobles that followed Malcolm
' 3d; nor the many prifoners taken by him,
' nor the 50 boroughs erected for the Englifh
' in Scotland, anno 1070; even though
' every family had one or two fervants from
' England : but it is the trade of all the *Scots*
' *Antiquifts* to fight againft all authority,
' truth, and common fenfe : one would
' have thought that fome one of them
' would have ftumbled on the truth ; I
' have already fhewn that the *Picts* were a
' Gothic people.' Then he goes on to
fhew the fuperiority of the Gothic tongue,
though he does not know five fentences of
it. But nothing is too arduous for him,
provided the *mobile vulgus* do but applaud

him

him for his ability at railing, (an excellent
quality commonly acquired at Billinfgate
and fuch other excellent feminaries of polite
learning;) as this gentleman hardly produces any thing that is new, but the fame
dull tautology conftantly ringing in our
ears; fo a man is afhamed to filence him
by urging always the like ufelefs round of
tautological arguments; a circumftance no
way pleafant to the judicious reader. We
muft then only obferve, that when a man
traduces a whole nation, he ought to ftand
upon firm ground, for fear of a fall; but
amidft fuch fcurrility of incoherent words,
there is not a fingle fact advanced to convince any man of the juftnefs of thefe unmannerly affertions; but what he produces
out of his own purfe, and therefore unworthy of a folid anfwer.

But as thefe fcurrilous effufions are poured
out upon a whole nation, by way of revenge
againft the two Macpherfons, the kind
reader is again intreated to indulge the author a little, while he rehearfes the advantages which the Rev. Dr. had from the
earlieft

earlieft period of life, refpecting his education. As for Mr. James, his works can
fpeak for him, and bear teftimony in his favour; and if he thinks that his character, as
a man of letters, will be affected by Mr. P.
he is alive and able to anfwer for himfelf.

But as the Dr. whom a worthy clergyman teftifies to have been a moft learned
and polite gentleman, whofe knowledge as
a fcholar, and elegance as an author, re-
flects much honour on his country, feeing
the Dr. I fay, is now dead, and cannot retort
on this enemy, the public may depend on
the following account to be ftrictly true.

This gentleman was born in Skye, fucceeded in his charge by his fon, who is the 7th
generation of minifters out of that family,
and I have authority to fay, that the firft of
them ranked among the Scottifh Bifhops.
Skye, is an ifland within one quarter of a
mile of Scotland, and not one of the 5
Ebudæ, as Mr. P. gives out. It is 54
computed, or 81 meafured miles in length,
and about 22 in breadth, extremely fertile,
and beautiful; ftored with the fineft marble

G 3 above

above ground, marls, minerals, foffils, coals, and fuller's earth, as remarked by John Smith, in his memoirs of the woollen manufactury in the fixteenth century, and may be dug 5 or 6 feet under the earth and fandy hillocks.

There are two great proprietors over this ifle, with many fine families of great vaffals, that in point of antiquity in that ifle will almoft vie with the Lords or Lairds to whom it belongs. Such as the leafeholders of *Elean Riabhoch, Cor Chatchan, Unifh, Ru, N-Dunan, Talifgear, Balmeanach, Ulinifh,* and many more. Some of the vaffals are Colonels, Majors, Captains, and Lieutenants. There are feven large parifhes fupplied by able clergymen. And even within ten miles only of this very populous ifle, one meets with two *Sheriff*-deputies, and 8 or 9 Juftices of the Peace, and a Baron Baillie, to keep up ftrict order ; and the reft of the ifland is equally well regulated.

The inhabitants, without exaggerating, are the moft hofpitable, converfable, and many of them the moft learned of any men

of

of equal number, from any country of the
fame extent in Great Britain—exclufive of
cities. It therefore can hardly be fuppofed
that in fuch a fociety books would be wanting.

That independent of the proprietors' libraries, they have, at leaft moft of them,
fine collections of books, which the author
affirms, from his own knowledge, and well
chofen too, in their private libraries. Mr.
Macpherfon had his education in the Great
academy of Skye, and was taught by his
uncle; who then had no fuperiors, and but
few equals in claffical knowledge in North
Britain.

And not a few of his old pupils, to fome
of them Dr. Johnfon bears teftimony of
their abilities, would compofe Latin verfes
that would not difhonour Buchanan, and an
epigram wrote by the Dr. is ftill extant,
that will almoft equal that gentleman's. It
cannot then be once imagined that the Dr.
with thefe early advantages on his fide, in
the happy neighbourhood of fo genteel and
learned a fociety of gentlemen, together

G 4   with

with his vicinity to Invernefs and Aberdeen, and the friendfhip which all the
Synod had for fo learned a man, would want
any book he judged convenient to call for;
and having at the fame time the libraries of
his predeceffors, with that of his father's,
his uncle's, and his own collection of books
at hand.

Thefe are only a few of the advantages
which the learned Dr. poffeffed; and yet
Mr. P. has repeatedly told his readers, that
his library was fmall, and his chance of acquiring knowledge limited. The malicious
treatment given to all the other highlanders
is beyond defcription erroneous. For it is
true, as Mr. James Macpherfon and every
gentleman, who have travelled that country,
acknowledges, that the extreme defire of
acquiring knowledge, even from travellers,
is perfectly juft. They will follow for a mile
any ftranger they fee on the road, and the
author has feen one of thefe farmers, even
in the midft of harveft, turn back with his
horfe and fledge, enquiring after news, and
returned perfectly fatisfyed with the information

mation given him, though at the expence
of his time, which might have been employed to better advantage; and this frank-
nefs in afking and giving news is accompanied with extreme modefty and good manners, and they are cautious of giving offence
to the ftrangers.

Even the weft Hebridians will immediately go on board every veffel that comes
into an harbour. And if long without feeing
veffels in their harbour to bring news, they
will at times go out to fea, after veffels that
are paffing by their coafts, for information;
and as moft of thefe poor men have fpent
much of their time either in the army, navy,
or mercantile line; fo it renders their converfation both agreeable and edifying; and
all thefe things principally arife from their
acute penetrating difpofition.

I am certain that it is not only invidious,
but dangerous, to run comparifons between
nations, and few men of real prudence will
be guilty of an offence fo obnoxious. Here,
however, the author is provoked to make
a ftretch, which otherwife his natural dif-

.   pofition

pofition would revolt at the very thought of. Then, though he was born within fight of Edinburgh, and of courfe as much of a low-lander, as a highlander, he avers that the inferior clafs of lowlanders, whom Mr. P. fo defignedly extols for their fuperiority, will fneak off the road to avoid a travelling ftranger; and fometimes, from blunt bafh-fulnefs, they will conceal themfelves behind a park, or hedge, until he paffes beyond their reach—and if he wants information, he muft follow after them.

And it is a certain fact, that the writer met with one man of this laft defcription in Fintry, a few miles from Kippen, in Dunbartonfhire, who could not inform, or direct him to the houfe of a gentleman of note, that had ftood for ages within fix miles of the place of his birth; and de-clared that he never heard of fuch a gentle-man, and bluntly told at parting, that the circle of his acquaintance had never ex-tended beyond the narrow limits of the parifh, church, and market. It is true, the commoners in general are more know-ing

ing than this laft mentioned, but ftill they have not the pleafing infinuating manner of the highlanders, much lefs their hofpitality; and had not Mr. P. been too much con-fined within the narrow walls of fome town or other, his ideas of the country people and their manners would lead him to ex-prefs himfelf more guardedly, and meafure merit more from the real, than imaginary actions of men.

In fupport of the advantages which Dr. Macpherfon received in his youth, we men-tion one Campbell, from Harris, who was *cotemporary*, and probably a clafs-compa-nion. This gentleman happened to vifit Edinburgh a few days before a great trial of candidates for filling a vacant chair in that renowned Univerfity came on. Many learned men came forward, and thefe recommended by high intereft, to difpute for fo valuable a prize. Among others, in fteps Campbell, though a mere ftranger and without friends, having only his Univerfity credentials to recommend him. One would imagine his chance was but fmall under thefe circumftances;

ftances; and yet how will Mr. P. ftare, when told that Campbell is reported to have gained the gown? *Nemine Contradicente.* And yet his volatile unfettled mind would not be bound down to the conftant drudgery of attendance. He therefore immediately refigned the office to the candidate, whofe merit placed him the next as beft qualified, faying, that the honour of fhewing what he could do, was all he required. This fact is faid to be undifputedly true.

Nay, this fame Campbell and another fchool-fellow, attempted boldly to introduce a new language in Skye, and they would converfe with each other for hours in it. And doubtlefs, had the people adopted it, we would be told by Mr. P. that it was the Pikifh tongue of old Scandinavia, which thefe learned men had preferved from oblivion.

This then was the country of Doctor Macpherfon; thefe were his advantages. Thefe alfo are the accomplifhments of the Gentlemen, with the natural fagacity of the commoners, or favages of Mr. P. in the high-

highlands and ifles ; and I challenge any
man of honour, if acquainted there, to
contradict the general truth of them. It
is granted there may be a few of Mr. P.'s
defcription, to be met with there, as well
as elfewhere ; but fuch unprincipled ex-
ceptionable characters are marked out, and
privately defpifed among the Gentlemen.
But let not my words alone decide this
matter. We fhall hear what Dr. Johnfon,
and others, who were known to be impartial critics, wrote on this head, and their
teftimonies cannot be doubted. Dr. Johnfon met with none of Mr. P's. favages, when
he fays, that a longer journey than to the
highlands muft be taken by the man, whofe
curiofity pants for favage virtues and barbarous grandeur.

  Such a feat of hofpitality as Raarfay, fills
the imagination with a delightful contrariety
of images ; without is the rough ocean,
the rocky land, beating billows, and howl-
ing ftorm ; within is plenty and elegance,
beauty and gaiety, the fong and the dance.
Our reception at Raarfay exceeded our expectation,

pectation ; we found nothing but civility; elegance, and plenty. The carpet was rolled off the floor ; the mufician was called, and the whole company was invited to dance ; nor did ever fairies trip with greater alacrity; the general air of feftivity which predominated in this place, fo far remote from all thofe which the mind has been ufed to contemplate in the manfions of pleafure, ftruck the imagination with delightful furprife, analagous to that which is felt at an unexpected emerfion from darknefs to light. When it was time to fup, fix and thirty perfons fat down to two tables, after which began the *Erfe* fongs. More gentlenefs of manners, nor a more pleafing appearance of domeftic fociety, is not found in the moft polifhed countries.

In Raarfay, if Mr. Johnfton could have found an Ulyffes, he had fancied a Phæacia. In fhort, fays he, J faw not one in all the ifles, whom I had reafon to think either deficient in learning, or irregular in life, but found feveral with whom I could not converfe, without wifhing as my refpects increafed,

increafed, that they had not been Prefby-
terians.

The converfation of the iflanders is in-
offenfive, and there is no difaffeétion at their
tables; I never heard a health offered by a
highlander, that might not be circulated
within the precinéts of the king's palace.

We fhall now hear Mr.Bofwell's account
of the highlanders. He tells us, that when
Dr. Johnfon was fo delighted with the
fcenes of elegance and entertainment he
met with at Raarfay, that he faid, I know
not how we fhall get away.

Here both make honourable mention of
Mr. Murchifon, faétor to Mac Leod at
Glenelg. When they paffed his houfe, un-
noticed by that gentleman, he fent a
bottle of rum and fugar to Dr. Johnfon and
Mr. Bofwell, as they could not be fo well
provided for at the ferry-houfe, where
they put up, and acquainted them in
his polite card, how forry he was that he
did not hear of them till they had paffed
his houfe; otherwife he would have in-
fifted on their paffing that night there.

Such

Such extraordinary attention from this gentleman to entire ſtrangers deſerves the moſt honourable commemoration; moſt gentlemen in the north-weſt of Scotland are of the ſame generous diſpoſition with this honourable man reſpecting hoſpitality; nay, and they are hurt when ſtrangers paſs by without giving them an opportunity of diſplaying marks of friendſhip and attention.

Dr. Johnſon was equally well pleaſed with his entertainment at Mr. Mackinnon's in Corichatchan in Sky, at Mr. Macdonald's, Kingſborrough, at Mr. Mac Leod's of Uliniſh, and at Dunvegan Caſtle; and ſaid there ſeemed to be no jealouſy, nor diſcord at Raarſay, and the gaiety of the ſcene was ſuch, that Mr. Boſwell himſelf doubted for a moment, whether unhappineſs had any place in that family.

Nor were they leſs ſatisfied at Talifgear : Colonel Mac Leod being bred to phyſic, had a tincture of learning which pleaſed Dr. Johnſon; he had ſome very good books; he remarked, that he had

found

found a library in his room at Talifgear;
and obferved, that it is one of the remarkable things of Sky, that there were fo
many books in every houfe he had vifited
in that ifle, and Colorel Mac Leod's lady
had all the polite refinement of the conti-
nent.

We fhall next hear the remarks made
on their learning. Being informed, fays
Mr. Bofwell, that the Rev. Mr. Donald
Mac Queen was the moft learned man in
Sky, and a cotemporary with Dr. Macpherfon; we were favoured with a letter
of introduction to him by the learned Sir
James Fowlis; we found him a decent old
man, with his own black hair, cautious
and rather flow of fpeech, but candid, fenfible, and well informed, nay, learned. Dr.
Johnfon was pleafed with him, and faid,
this is a critical man, Sir, there muft be great
vigour of mind, to make him cultivate learning fo much in the ifle of Sky, where he
might do without it. It is wonderful how
many of the new publications he has. His
brother was the fourth generation of mini-

H   fters

.fters of his familiy in the parifh of Snifort, and both of them joined and bought books from time to time; fuch books as had reputation.

Mr. Mac Queen repeated paffages of Offian, out of the original, and told Dr. Johnfon that he heard his grandfather had a copy of it; but that he could not affirm that Offian had compofed all that poem, as it is now publifhed; but Johnfon contended againft the authenticity of it, and maintained that as good an epic ode could have been compofed out of the old fongs of Robinhood, as out of Offian's; fuch was his prejudice againft the production, that he would rather allow Macpherfon to poffefs the honour of that performance, than agree to its antiquity, a few paffages excepted.

At Oftig, the Rev. Dr. Macpherfon's own houfe, he found a clofet ftored with books, Greek, Latin, French, and Englifh belonging to the learned doctor, a man of diftinguifhed talents; Dr. Johnfon looked alfo at a Latin paraphrafe of the Song of Mofes written by him, and publifhed 1747

in.

in a Magazine of June, and faid it does him great honour, he has a great deal of Latin, and good Latin too, continues he. The Dr. read another *Latin ode* which he wrote when minifter of Barra, where he refided for fome years, and thought himfelf buried alive among barbarians, efteeming that ifle inferior to Sky, his *natale folum*, that he lan-guifhed for its bleffed mountains.

Hei mihi; quantos patior dolores,
Dum procul fpecto, juga ter beata
Dum færæ Barræ fteriles arenas
     Solus aberro.

Ingemo, indignor, crucior quod inter
Barbaros Thulen lateam colentes.
Torpeor languens, morior fepultus
     Carcere cæco.

After wifhing for wings to fly over to his dear country which was in his view, from what he calls *Thule*, as being the moft wef-tern ifle of Scotland, except *St. Kilda*; and after defcribing the pleafures of fociety, and

      the

the miferies of folitude, he at laft, with a
becoming propriety, has recourfe to the only
fure relief of thinking men; *furfum corda,*
the hope of a better world, and difpofes his
mind to refignation.

Interim fiat tua, rex, voluntas
Erigor furfum quoties fubit fpes,
Certa migrandi folimam fupernam,
Numinis aulam.

And he concludes with a noble ftrain of
orthodox piety.

Vita dum demum vocitanda vita eft
Tunc licet gratos focios habere,
Seraphim et fanctos triadem verendam,
Concelebrantes.

It is to be feared that Mr. P. even with
the aid of Jeffrey of Monmouth, would
not half equal this beautiful Saphic ode—
Ah! Pinkerton, Pinkerton!—for fhame!—
here is much more learning than expected.

The

The Dr. when taking leave of thefe people, faid he fhould never forget Sky, and returned thanks for all their civilities to him. Mr. Buchanan regrets much that Mr. P. was not of that party; in which cafe, he believes, we would have heard nothing of Celtic favages.

The friendly attention paid to them by the young Laird of Coll, who accompanied them from Sky, when they arrived at his houfe, in the ifland of Coll, was fingularly kind. The Dr. paid a vifit to the Rev. Hector Mac Lean, of *Coll* and *Tyree*. This gentleman being about 77 years of age, a decent ecclefiaftic, dreffed in a full fuit of black, and had as much dignity as the Dean of a Cathedral in his appearance; he was learned, and had a valuable library, as the Dr. writes.

The minifters in the iflands, and highlands, had attained fuch knowledge as may juftly be admired in men who have no motive to ftudy; but generous curiofity, or what is ftill better a defire of ufefulnefs, with fuch politenefs as fo narrow a circle of

converfe

converfe could not have fupplied, but to minds difpofed to elegance.

Says Mr. Bofwell, we were a night elegantly entertained at the houfe of the Rev. Mr. Niel M'Leod, in Mull; and Dr. Johnfon faid, that he was the cleareft headed man that he had met with in the weftern ifles; even though they had from time to time their intelligence facilitated, and their converfation enlarged by the company of the learned Mr. M'Queen, minifter in Skye; whofe knowledge and politenefs gave him a title equally to kindnefs and refpect. ' Indeed, the civilities,' fays the Dr. ' that we met with at every place would be ungrateful to omit, and tedious to repeat, during the courfe of our travels in the Hebrides.'

So much for the better fort of the natives : we fhall take the Dr.'s opinion of the inferior clafs, feeing that alfo may be depended upon, from his mouth, being naturally difpofed againft partiality in their favour, without juft reafon to prompt him to it. Both the highland fervants whom we hired from Invernefs gave fatisfaction, being civil and

ready-

ready-handed. ' Civility,' fays he, ' feems part
of the national character ; every chieftain is
a monarch ; and politenefs, the natural
product of royal government, is diffufed
from the laird to the whole clan.

Were I a chief, I would drefs my fervants better than myfelf, and knock a fel-
low down, if he looked faucy to a Mac
Donald in rags ; but I would not treat men
as brutes. I would let them know why all
my clan were to have attention paid to them ;
I would tell my upper fervants why, and
make them tell it to others.' Here the Dr.
would act like a man of honour and humanity; and it is a pity that Mr. P. had not
difcovered the fame benevolence to the clans
fo much injured by him. The above, it is
hoped, is fufficient to convince him of his
ill-judged afperity, and in fome future performance will force an apology for it, and
impute the whole to his ignorance of their
real worth.

We now leave with any gentleman of
candour and humanity to judge of the man,
who would out-face truth fo unguardedly

H 4   by

by his abuſe of a whole people, ſo brave as
the highlanders are known to be, and that
without provocation given.

'In the cold climate of Scandinavia,' ſays
Mr. P. 'the people did, as they ſtill do,
'delight in gutturals and dentals: the cli-
'mate has rendered their organs rigid and
'contracted; and cold makes them keep
'their mouths ſhut as much as poſſible.'
This is a ſtrange account given of the
Piks; if true, they remind us of the Tro-
glodytes mentioned by Xenophon, who burrowed under ground, and ſpoke through
their throats like ſea-gulls.

That ſame account is ſufficient to convince people that the Scots PECHS had
not the moſt diſtant connection with ſuch
beings. On the contrary, *Tacitus* tells us,
that, after the learned and eloquent ſpeech
delivered by *Galcacus*, ſo far from keeping
their mouths ſhut, they opened them with a
mighty ſhout of applauſe: *Excipere ora-*
tionem alacres, et barbari mores cantu et
fremitu clamoribuſque diſſonis. Here the
whole mouths of theſe formidably, fierce,

jarring

jarring people are widely opened, finging and fhouting aloud, and no fear of cold air among thofe brave hoftile heroes. Befides, they received the epithet PECHS from their labour and induftry, as appeared from their workmanfhip. But the country of Scandinavia was fo barren, that cultivation of the ground did not employ any part of their time fo early. In every point of view Mr. P. will fail in his attempt to make the knowing world believe the Scots PECHS were defcended from thefe PIKS.

Mr. P. leaves people in the dark with regard to the origin of the name *Pik*. But we can affure the reader, that the PECHS from Scotland received their name from labour and induftry, and by no means from the Roman *Picti*; for painting the fkin was peculiar to many other nations under different names. Nor did they derive their *Agnomen* from the PICHTIDH of Dr. Macpherfon, or plunderers,; for that epithet in all confcience was more applicable to the Scots (than to the *Picts*) who, according to himfelf, thought no fhame of the profeffion,

feffion, provided they had the judgment to form, with the fpirit and addrefs to execute it with fafety.

The name was ironically given them by their Scots neighbours, who looked upon all kind of manual labour as unworthy of gentlemen; and oft preferred the plunder-ing of the induftrious PECHS of the fruits of their labour, to the hard drudgery of earning their own bread by the fweat of their brows.

In common converfation they are called PECHS (not *Picts*) in Scotland, the very name in *Gaelic* given to working people to this day. *Caid mibhel no* PEICH, or PEICHIN ? Where are the labourers, or workers? *Garim no* PEICH *ntaobh fho*, Call the labourers this way—is the lan-guage of a mafter, or overfeer, through all the north-weft Hebrides; fo that the name PECH is always known to fignify workers, where the language is well known and un-derftood. As when a poor drudge in Harris is wore out with labour, the only fure te-nure by which he can be allowed to keep his
little

little roof over his head in one place, he be-
moans his own cafe by faying, *chá nurni
fa pheigh mi ni sfaid*—I am incapable to labour any longer. *Ha m-peigh ar mo chuir a
dhi*—the work has killed me. *Co heafas
fa pheigh as mo leidh*—Who will ftand out
to work for me?

The firft natural implement of hufbandry
is the *Piȼt* axe to dig up ftones, and clear
the ground of trees and roots, and to level
heights and rugged fpots. And in Gaelic,
this tool is called PECHD or PECHAD, and
thofe who work with it are nominated
Peichs, PEICHARIN. And to this day in
Harris, the poor labourers make ufe of it;
being themfelves almoft in a ftate of nature, and their plantations nearly in the
fame ftate. And with this rude implement
almoft every fpecies of work is carried on
by thefe people.

With a fmall and lighter kind of
PECHD, their potatoes are digged up inftead of ufing fpades, the *rue* for dying red
colour, and the *tormentil* roots for barking
and tanning their leather are picked out of
the

the ground; with the fame inftrument they
raife their dung, and fill their panniers and
creels out of their houfes, with a fimilar
implement in one hand commonly the fea
ware is raifed, and they hand it into
their panniers, which they carry from the
fhore to their fields; and alfo a root called
Brifgian, Maftroot, which the poor natives
frequently ufe inftead of potatoes in time of
fcarcity; in fine, with it they fharpen their
quern ftones, with many other purpofes to
which it is employed, juft as the old
PECHS on the eaft of Scotland did when in
the fame infancy of hufbandry, as may be
traced from analogy; and therefore might
juftly be named, though ironically, from
their implements of farming by their Scotch
neighbours, who had not in thefe early
times begun to plant their ground with
corn or barley for the fupply of the necef-
faries of life. This is the true and moft
rational origin of that name, and not *Piɛ̃ts*,
from painting their fkins, a circumftance
common to them with many other other
people

people as well as the Scots, though not fo
named, from their not ufing the PECHD.

Some are of opinion, that the Picts were
originally Germans, that they came to Britain from Denmark, others derive them
from the *Pictones* in France; others from
the Scythians, or Thracians; and in fine,
others contend, with more propriety, that
they were Britons, that they they fpoke
the fame language, had much the fame
laws, cuftoms and manners, and were by
foreigners only called *Picti*. ' For,' fays
Abercrombie, ' what appellations they took
to themfelves before then, no author relates; 'and he is of this opinion himfelf, and
firmly believes, that the Scots and Irifh
were alfo Britons, and that they, as alfo
did the *Picts*, came, but in after ages, by
their denominations, becaufe the Scots highlanders to this day, neither defign themfelves, nor thofe that inhabit the lower
parts of the country, *Scots* (though fure
enough true SCOTCH.)

But the name was not recited nor current
till the days of Claudian, or rather before
his

his time, as he flourished about the year
390. And he takes it for granted that
they were the same people, though they
were divided by factions and tribes, and
gave obedience to different Princes, with
their various and ever jarring interests.

The Scots and *Picts*,' continues the same
author, ' were so nearly allied to one another by blood, religion, laws, language, and
neighbourhood, had, while they dreaded
any danger from the South Britains or Romans, continued to cultivate a strict and
inviolate friendship, till the reign of Crathilinthus king of the Scots, in whose time
they quarrelled about a hunting dog, which
some *Picts* of the domestics, or retinue of
the king THELARGUS, had stollen from a
domestic servant of *Crathilinthus*. From
this trifling circumstance, says Buchanan, a
bloody national war broke out between
them.

This happened anno 273. But by the
mediation of *Carusius*, and some others, a
peace was made at this time; but it broke
again

again in the year 348, and thus both nations continued quarrelling until the grand
Revolution, or rather total eclipfe of the
Scottifh Monarchy was affected about the
year 359, as obferved elfewhere,

This being 689 years after Fergus the
Firft, 413 after the firft entrance of Ju-
liu⁹ Cæfar into the ifland, and 275 years
after the full conqueft of South Britain by
Agricola in the days of Domitian.

Sir James Lauderdale remarks, that the
Scots alfo were underftood by the name
Piĉts, whom king Kenneth had fubdued
anno 875, in Cumberland, efpecially when
he afferts, that Edward the Firft, fon to
king Alfred, had the kings of the Cem-
brians, Scots, the Streg-welfh fubjects
to him as their fuperior Lord; fo that
thofe who in king Alfred's time were called
Piĉts, were in king Edward's time called
Scots. Sir James ftrains every nerve to
annihilate the name of the *Piĉts*, though it
is certain from other hiftorians, as well as
common fenfe, that they were *Piĉts*, and
not Scots, who inhabited Cumberland. For
the

the Scots had no time to fettle in that country fo early after Kenneth M'Alpin's conqueft; and if they had, they would not
have rebelled againft their benefactor a
few years only after tafting of his favours;
but they were the difcontented *Picts* who
fpurned at the government of the Scots king
over them. And whatever part the *Picts*
had in Cumberland fell to the Scots, by the
deed of king Edmund's to Malcolm in 945;
being only a confirmation rather than a new
grant, efpecially feeing Ingulphus, in his
account of the battle of Brunford in 938,
among thofe who fought with Conftantine
king of the Scots, againft king Altheftane,
he mentions Eugenius king of the Cembri,
which was a very common name in Scotland, and of which we had many kings;
and there never have been any Welch king
of that name known to us. It is almoft
certain that Bede thought the *Picts* and
Scots were one people, or at leaft nearly
connected. Thefe unconquered nations,
againft whom Severus built the wall be-
twixt Clyde and Forth, whom he reckoned
the

the ancient inhabitants of the ifland, before
the arrival of the Romans, and did not think
their firft arrival in the ifland was, (as others
foolifhly do) in the time of Maximus the
tyrant, when the firft of the three vaftations
of the Britons began : but as thefe vaftations
ended the war with the Scots, and Piéts ;
when the Britons were expelled the north
as foon as the Romans left it. So that the
Scots and Piéts were no otherwife *Trans-
marines*, but as they were feparated from the
Britons, by the Forth, and Clyde Friths,
with the wall of Severus, which made, as it
were, a kind of ifland, as Tacitus remarks.
Bede calls both *indomite gentes*, unfubdued
people. Nennius alfo, fpeaking of them;
calls them *Piéts* and *Scots* jointly ; *quia
Piéti ab aquilone, et Scoti, ab occidente una-
nimiter pugnabant contra Britones.* The
Piéts from the north, and the Scots from
the weft, fought unanimoufly againft the
Britons ; this clearly points out their natural conneétion, and their antiquity in Scotland ; fo that Bede was in the right in
writing, that all the inhabitants of Britain

I   were

were *indigenes*, that is, fprung up in the country; and none of them either *Piɛts* or *Scots*,
lately arrived, as fome vain fanciful hiftorians have, without good authority, afferted: *omnem aquilonarum extremam infulæ
partem pro indigenis ad murum ufque capef-
funt*, namely, that the northern inhabitants,
whether Piɛts or Scots, both being from
the fame origin, feized upon the country,
as far as the wall, meaning the wall of
Hadrian, as juftly obferved by Sir James
Lauderdale, feeing that of Severus confined
them within the ifle; but now they are broke
out beyond thefe limits and advanced farther
fouth; indeed the confufed account, which
Camden gives us the country of the Piɛts,
and Scots, not only marks their profeffion
as farmers or PEICHS, but alfo their affinity
with the Scots; and Sir James Lauderdale
likewife writes, that the *Piɛts* poffeffed
from Galloway to Lothian, and from thence
over Forth and Tay, to the Orkney and
Shetland ifles, called Pentland Firth (from
the *Piɛts*;) and when the limits of the nation were extended in Northumberland,
the

the Picts went into the fouth, and inhabited moft parts of the conqueft towards England, (leaving the northern parts to the
Scots) as being more fit for labour, having
their royal feat at Abbernethy. They left
the Scots to enlarge their poffeffions, as far
as the weftern fhires of Galloway, and
and northwards in the highlands towards
Invernefs; lands only fit for pafture. Thus
we find that the richeft countries are allowed to be the property of the *Picts*, becaufe
hufbandry was their profeffion, from which
the *Agnomen* was given them, and it is ftill
fo applied in Gaelic; while the Scots are
faid to live by pafturage of cattle, fifhing,
and hunting, a profeffion more adapted to
their genius, and from which they alfo derived the nick-name *Scode*. As the Picts
had always the country, it evidently points
out that they were the oldeft, or parents,
and the Scots, the younger people, and defcended from them.

Sir Robert Sibbald, who wrote about the
beginning of this century, muft alfo give his
opinion of the Picts and Scots, although

equally

equally ignorant of the Celtic tongue with moft other authors; and his fentiments in order to make the Picts a Gothic people, he draws in Buchanan among the firft to affift him. The opinion of Buchanan, fays he, was that the Picts were Goths, efpecially that tribe of them, of which *Argachocoxus* was the chief; for he poffeffed the country of Fife: but we find that Buchanan only imagines they were Scythians or Germans, not Goths, as at that time the inhabitants of Scandia were underftood to be; *cum Picti ferre cutem variarent, ac diverforum anima-. lium figuris infcriberent veriis erit quærere quæ gentes vel in Scythia, vel Germania regionibus, &c.*

It is admitted, that in a more extenfive point of view, fome have maintained that Denmark and Norway were included; but that does not prove that the Picts were Goths, unlefs the whole Germans were fuch, which proves too much. On the contrary, the language fpoke by both difproves the affertion.

Alfo

Alfo, Buchanan's argument of the Picts
cutting figures on their bodies, is not more
applicable to the Goths, than to many other
nations; neither does Mr. Maule's *Coch*,
that is, red, *in arguntocoxus*, add ftrength to
it; becaufe the word was unknown to the
Picts; for the red colour is exprefled in Gaelic, (the language of the *Picts*) by the epi-
that *dearag*, or *ruo*, which fully exprefles the
idea of the colour; thus Sir Robert Sibbald
thinks he has fully proved his point; but he
finds himfelf oppofed by Sir Will. Temple
concerning the origin of the *Picts*, in regard
he brings even the Scots from Scythia,
which Sir Robert denies, in as much as moft
of the ancient and modern hiftorians agree,
that the Scots came from Spain, and not
from Scythia, and is offended with Sir Will.
Temple, for miftaking the Scots for the
Picts; but Sir Wiliam's argument proves
the affinity between thefe people; and he
alfo maintains, that the north weft of Scotland, as well as Ireland, were called Jerne,
and that the Scots afterward divided into two
nations; thofe of the eaft called themfelves

I 3   Scots

Scots Alabinich, and the reſt who poſſeſſed the weſt ſide, were called Scots Erin; and at whatever period it was, it is agreed that they ſubdued moſt of the country on their firſt entrance into Caledonia, and mingled with the reſt of the native Piĉts. They both continued long to infeſt the frontier parts of the Roman colonies in Britain, with great fiercenefs; and many various events; and would probably have made much greater noiſe, and impreſſion on the Romans, if the greater number had not been drawn over to Ireland by ſo great a drain, which they totally conquered, and long poſſeſſed.

Sir William differs quite from others reſpeĉting the Scots, and the population of Ireland; and his conjeĉture is no wife improbable, nor impoſſible to be nearer the truth concerning Ireland than Sir Robert's, with ancient and modern hiſtorians, who join in ſentiments with him.

From all of which it appears, that Mr. Pinkerton is not ſingular in his conjeĉture concerning the Piĉts of Scandinavia being the

the anceftors of the Scots Piɛts, and he only joins them in their miftake.

When undifputed authority cannot be
produced, every man is left at liberty to form
conjeɛtures for himfelf; and each generally
define fuch *epithets* as they handle according
to the language beft underftood by them,
whether agreeable to the fubjeɛt which originally give them birth, or not; thus the
Romans knew of no word more like *Pechs*
than *Piɛti*, and Mr. P. knows of no Gothic
term more anfwerable than Piks, yet without
once informing us, what thefe Piks meant
in that language, or anfwering why it was
applied to fuch people, he gives out that
thefe were anceftors of the *Pechs*. I am
well aware that the fame objeɛtion may be
ftated againft my own account alfo, as being
only a conjeɛture ; but I affirm that the
living language places what I have faid beyond a conjeɛture, and eftablifhes a pofitive
proof of its certainty—and had other competent judges of the Gaelic language reflected ferioufly, they had made the fame remarks
on the expreffion, as it marks out in forci-
ble

I 4

ble terms the very object which gave rife to the *agnomen*, particularly as the *Celtic* tongue is unalterable, and the terms ufed by the Romans, are as well known now, as they were then to the natives; and it is a weak argument which Sir Robert Sibbald ufes to convince the inquifitive reader, that the Goths were the Picts, merely becaufe old Anglo-Saxon Scoticifms are to be met with through Fife, and along the German coaft, on the fouth of the Humber.

For the word Fife itfelf is Gaelic, and is not derived from Fifus, or Veach; and moft names of ancient places over all Fife is well known to be Gaelic, and were affixed long there; and in moft places over all Britain before ODIN, the laft king of that name, with his Goths came to Scandia, as that time is pretty well known, or even before the Saxons were heard of. Procopius alfo, who writes the hiftory of the Goths, gives an account of a conference between *Belifarius* and fome of the Gothic ambaffadors, who were fent to him, and from this fpeech Sir Robert Sibbald takes occafion to announce, that the

Picts

P.cts were Goths, but with little fhow of
reafon, as appears from the words themfelves. The Goths fay, *Siciliam tantam
tamque divitem vobis permittimus, infulam,
fine qua ne quidem, Affrica tuta poffeffio.
Nos inquit, Belifarius, vero Britanicum haud
paulo majorem Sicilia et Romani antiquitas
juris largimur Gothis.* Now, fays Sir Robert
Sibbald, where were the Goths in Britain
which Belifarius fpeaks of, if they were not
the *Picts*?

Here the Baronet, to ferve his purpofe,
makes a large ftride in favour of the Goths ;
for, *largimur Gothis* may rationally be
taken in the fame fenfe with *Siciliam permittimus Romanis*, that is to fay, we Goths
make over Sicily to the Romans, or to you
in their name ; and the gcneral, on the other
hand, beftows Britain on the Goths, whom
the ambaffador reprefented ; not that thc
Goths were then in poffeffion, but might
come after the agreement was ratified ; befides Belifarius could only mean a part, not
the whole of Britain, as it would be abfurd
to imagine that the Romans would make

over

over two kingdoms for the paultry ifle of Sicily, he therefore only means the Ork-ney, or Long Ifland in the Hebrides, either of them were equal in extent to the ifle of Sicily, and which the Goths frequently invaded, and fometimes pofleffed them for a time; neither of which, properly fpeaking were valuable to the Picts, and not fo much occupied as the eaft were by thefe people. Hence we may conclude, that Sir Robert is in a miftake refpecting the meaning of the fentence, and that the *Picts* are not underftood to be Goths by this tranfaction of *Belifarius*, much lefs did they fpeak the fame language.

And this is not the firft inftance which might be pointed out, where authors, ancient as well as modern, have either perverted, or mifunderftood the fubjects they handled.

For *Tacitus*, who is almoft looked upon as the fure ftandard to be depended upon by moderns, hath erred, from mifinformation, or ignorance, as already in part remarked above, when treating of the expedition of Agricola, and even confeffed by himfelf; he

tells,

tells, cap. 45. that Agricola was dead four
years before he wrote his account of the
fixth year's expedition of his father-in-law
into Caledonia, and that he had his information from thofe who ferved under him, and
had not marked the circumftances of time
exactly.

For Agricola, in his fpeech before the laft
battle with Galgacus, fays, that it was the
eighth year; *Octavus annus eft commilliones*,
&c. of his expedition; and therefore the
fight in his camp, behoved to be on the
feventh year, yet Tacitus places it on the
fixth year, cap. 26. *cum interim*, *&c.* This
marks out how cautioufly we ought to read
his followers in all points, when he himfelf
hath been mifled.

Agricola, being apprehenfive of a general
infurrection in this large and remote country beyond the Forth, fent forth a fleet, as
above remarked, to try the creeks and ha-
vens of that extenfive country, on the fixth
year of his lieutenancy, where the *amplas
civitates* were (arifing fecretly from the antiquity of its inhabitants, who had long time

to

to enlarge them) ; and Julius Cæfar confirms
this truth in his Gallic war, lib. 5. when he
mentions the antiquity of the inhabitants of
north Britain, who, he fays, were fo ancient
that they thought themfelves they were
the *Aborigines.* Diodorus Siculus, in his
Bibliotheca, is of the fame opinion : and
Eumeneus the panegyrift, preferreth the actions of Conftantine in Britain, to the exploits of Caefar. He fheweth that the Picts
were in Britain long before Ceafar's time,
in thefe words : *natio etiam adhuc rudis et foli Britanni, Pictis modo, et Hibernis affueta
hoftibus adhuc feminudis, &c.* When Beda
writes that the Picts came from Scythia,
and this affirmed by Mathew of Weftminifter and many others, yet, fays Sir Robert Sib
bald we are to underftand the European, and
not the Afiatic Scythia ; the Baronet gives
it this term, left the PECHS fhould be older than the late Goths ; but we muft allow
Beda to mean the northern Afiatic Scythians;
feeing, according to Pliny, lib. 6. cap. 13.
ab extrimo aquilone is mentioned, and lib. 4
cap. 12. he adds, that the Gætæ, Daci, and
Sarmatæ

Sarmatæ, and even the Germans, were called Scythians, and it is not doubted but
thefe came from Afia originally; in one
word, the more one fearches after the truth
among the different, difagreeing authors,
the more he perplexes himfelf, and muft
leave others uncertain who to rely upon
among fo many diverfified opinions; it is
therefore more fafe to rely on common fenfe,
the conftant practice of both *Picts* and *Scots*,
who agree in their manner, in almoft all circumftances, with a ftrong fupport of a living ancient language to illuftrate what
otherwife might for ever lie buried in oblivion; before we depend on men who are
ftrangers to that tongue, without which we
cannot hit upon the real truth concerning
thefe ancient people.

Befides, no other confiftent account can
be agreed upon among hiftorians, nor the
place from whence fuch people could come
to north Britain, with even probable certainty, as moft of them difagree in this particular : for we have already feen what Beda
and others fay. Beda, in his ecclefiaftical hiftory

tory maintains, that they came from Scythia firft to Ireland; Tacitus conjectures they came from Germany; Stillingfleet, in his Origin of Britain *, pretends to bring the Caledonians from Scandinavia; and Camden himfelf differs from Bede †, by faying, that the language of the *Piêts* was a daughter of the Germans, and Mr. P. brings the *Piks* of Norway (inftead of the PECHS) from the northern country. In the midft of fuch jarring diverfity of opinions, and each party judging themfelves in the right, though all of them equally remote from certainty, whether in this cafe is it not the fafeft mode (as above) to rely on the firm fupport, the prefent practice and living language of a people, who moft undoubtedly derived both from their anceftors, the ancient PECHS of Caledonia; for thefe were not named *Piêts*, but PECHS, as they ftill are from their implements of labour, the above PECHDAD in particular; rather than hunt up and down, through all Europe, and Afia, in fearch of an imaginary people, no where to be met with any

* Page 446. † Page 1468.

degree

degree of probability, much lefs of certainty that can afford a fatisfaction to an inquifitive mind in fearch of truth to reft upon.

The *Agathyrfi* from Scythia painted their fkins, as did the *Arii*, the *Geloni*, the *Scythi*, yet none of them were called Picts; *cæterum Ariique, &c.* *

Camden, at length, thinks that the *Picts* were the fame people with the Britons. If he does not mean the Welch, he is in the right, for the language and native hatred which formely fubfifted between the Welch and native Picts plainly indicate them a feparate people ; and Father Innis attempts to prove that they are the fame people (*i. c.* the PICTS) with the ancient Caledonians.

Nay, among the vulgar, common tradition confirms this ; they imagine that the Pechs, though invifible by day to men, could perform any hard piece of labour, as thrafhing, or building walls, and houfes, or any difficult job, by day light, only for the paultry reward of a little food left for them in fome

* Tacitus, Cap. 43.

fecret

fecret place, with proper inftructions, and fuppofed to be heard by the poor Pechs; this faint idea of their ingenuity goes a great length to eftablifh the above facts, even though none of their labour had reached our times.

In latter times the Pechs were called *Brownies*, in Gælic *Broinech*, filly people, a kind of Sorners (*Cernachs*), for concealing themfelves under caves like foxes, that infefted the country, and forcing honeft men to feed them with the beft provifion in their houfes; and on that account were a terror; and the name, though corrupted, continued to alarm the vulgar; in the Hebrides thefe are called *Gruagaichs Gruagfeachd*, a hairy-headed banditti, or a force of men, without caps or bonnets, who concealed themfelves in fecret glens and woods all day, and broke in upon defencelefs inhabitants to prey on their means, as opportunity offered; and the name of that band of robbers is a terror even to this day, and the credulous affrighted perfon gives out that the *Gruagach* is ftill at times feen in wild dangerous defarts.

Mr.

Mr. Martin calls thefe *Brownies,* fturdy *furies,* who, if they were fed and kindly treated, would do a great deal of work; ' but now,' fays Johnfon, ' they pay them no wages, they are content to labour for themfelves.'

Along with thefe different names they were, in after ages, called *Gruinnich,* in Gaelic, *Cruinneach,* affemblies, from their meeting together at any publick occafion either for war, or any other neceffary employment; thefe appellatives were, and are ftill given to the PEIGHS, according to the countries they refided in, and the neceffitous circumftances they were forced to affume; if they met with friendfhip, they became ufeful members of fociety, if not, they were forced to become hoftile.

The PEICHS, at leaft their defcendants, are ftill in North Britain, and they were never totally deftroyed; as fome writers foolifhly affirm them to have been all cut off by Kenneth Mac Alpin, who fubdued thefe people, and united them, and their kingdom to that of his original Scots dominion; but the PEICHS were a formidable people

K   long

long after this period, as may be seen from what they spake at the battle of Standard, from the following account: About the year 1138 old Robert the Bruce, grandfather to Robert, the king of Scotland, was so hurt at the dreadful ravages, which the country people sustained by these wars, that he melted into tears, when pleading with the king, to compassionate the melancholy circumstances of his subjects, and to put a period to it, insomuch that king David himself was much moved by his intercession before the battle of Standard was fought, and almost dreaded the consequences of a shameful retreat, in case he was worsted by the enemy, which actually happened as the good old gentleman foresaw. Those who maintain that all the Picts were destroyed by Kenneth Mac Alpin, a circumstance very improbable, and would, if true, be equally impolitic in a wise conqueror, they do not advert that the Picts of Galloway were so powerful at this period, (near 200 years after the overthrow of the Pictish kingdom) that they insisted on the right-

hand

hand, and claimed it as their right over the
Scots, being always their right according to
their ancient cuſtoms ; but though the king
was obliged to grant their demands, yet
they loſt the victory, becauſe they were ſo
much elated after their ſuccefs at the battle
of Clitherow, that they over-valued their
own prowefs, and defpiſed the enemy too
raſhly. It is remarkable, ſays Dalrymple,
that the different Engliſh hiſtorians calls
theſe men of Galloway, *Picti, Scoti, Gal-
wenſis, Loenenſis* *, *in fronte belli erant
Picti* †. *Acres Loenenſium qui gloriam pre-
mi ſitus, a rege Scotorum invito præripue-
rent* ‡. Thus we find that David king of
the Scots, was forced againſt his inclination
to yield their ancient right of leading the army into battle, a plain proof that the Picts
were very powerful at that time, and that
the Scots were only mixed with the Picts,
who ſtill remained in their old poſſeſſions in

* T. Haguſtald, page 262.
† Page 322.
‡ Huntington, page 288.

K 2   the

the fouth, and by no means totally diftroyed by Kenneth Mac Alpin, about the year 838.

‘ Mr. P. maintains that no Druids inha-
‘ bited beyond the prefent north Wales on the
‘ north, and the Garone, the boundaries of
‘ the Celtic *Gauls*, in the fouth.' He muft not however imagine that people will be fo condefcending as to believe his *ipfe dixit* alone, againft all traditions, and the prefent common language of Scotland, that mention the large and leffer circles of large erect-ed maffy ftone temples of the Druids; and even the prefent Chriftian churches in the highlands are named *Clachinn*, after thefe ftone buildings called *Druidical* places of worfhip; and going to church is commonly expreffed in Gaelic, *bhel u dol don Chlachan*, literally, are you going to the ftones, and not *bhel u dol don Eaglaifh*, (*i. e.* church).

Had Mr. P. feen and heard the awful refpect paid to thefe noble monuments, he certainly would have expreffed himfelf lefs dogmatically on that head. *Tacitus* mentions

tions the *Druids* of the ifle of Mann, and it
is certain the fame religion extended over
all the other Hebrides, of which MONA
was the fouthernmoft. Tacitus reprefents
the women, as acting the part of furies in
defence of their religion and temples : *in mo-*
dum furiarum vefti ferali crinibus dejeѐis fa-
cæs preferebant, Druideque circum preces
diras ad cælum manibus fublatis, fundentes ;
and had Tacitus feen the four grand temples
at Callarifh in *Lewis,* he would have left
an elegant defcription of thefe unequalled
piles.

But it is a great misfortune to North Britain, that there, as well as in all other places on the north-weft, almoft all the authors who have attempted to hand down
this hiftory to pofterity, were ftrangers to
the places, and depended too much on mifinformed authority, and of courfe the whole
of them have fallen fhort of the truth; nay,
even the Welch, and Irifh, as well as Englifh have failed egregioufly in this particular.

Thefe indeed attempt to give an account
of the eaft fide where the fcene of action

K 3   lay,

lay; but for the north-weft, their inteli-
gence is uncertain, and equally inaccurate,
owing to their ignorance of the country, being both remote, and forbidding,
and of courfe in their eye lefs interefting.

This was particularly the cafe with *Tacitus*,
who neither vifited, nor lived in Britain,
though he writes thus ignorantly from Italy.
He is the univerfal ftandard of appeal refpecting the hiftory of Britain; how would any
modern Italian be laughed at, if in this age
he attempted any fuch, and yet his information might be as perfect as that delivered
to Tacitus, or even to Cæfar, who never
travelled north of London for perfonal information.

And what then can be expected from authors lefs accurate, and many of them more
ignorant, and worfe informed, for want of
proper information; while the fame language that taught Cæfar, and afterwards
Tacitus to give the information, fuch as
they handed down to us, is not only defpifed
now, though the fame as then, but the very
people, who have preferved this noble monu-
ment

ment of their antient antiquity, and that too
for the honour of Britain, alive, are called favages, for this piece of good fervice, by Mr. P.
and even overlooked by fuch as ought to have
dealt more tenderly by them. But for any
thing *Tacitus* fays to the contrary, we may
fafely affirm, that *Druidifm* was as firmly e-
ftablifhed over all Britain, as the Chriftian
religion is at this day over the faid country :
it is therefore folly to argue againft any perfon that denys an opinion almoft fo univerfally received, and impoffible to be over-
thrown by rational principles, and found argument. ' The Celts', fays Mr. P. ' from
' all ancient accounts, as well as prefent
' knowledge, were, and are a favage race,
' incapable of labour, or even rude arts, as
' are the Fins.'

This railing man produces none of thefe
inftances or authorities in fupport of this
malevolent charge ; an infult to a whole nation, and fo contradictory to the general
known character of thefe brave people, in
whatever department they have been employed, whether religious, civil, or military.

K 4   The

The Celts on all occafions on the contrary, have difplayed uncommon abilities, and have been allowed to excel either in the pulpit, at the bar, or on military expeditions, and the province of phyfic and hiftory is in a manner given up to them.

After the rebellion forty-five, that great ftatefman the late Earl of Chatham underftood that, in order to ftrengthen the hands of government, it became neceffary, not only to knock of the fetters with which the former miniftry had impoliticly bound up thofe haughty inhabitants, than which nothing could be more improper, as was formerly remarked by Caftelnau, the Frenchman, who, in the time of the queen regent of Scotland, had much opportunity to penetrate into the real genius and difpofition of thefe people, and pointed out the manner of gaining upon them, that their affections and loyalty might be fecured. He fhewed the difficulty of forcing fuch men, as the Scots, to act contrary to their confciences. ' They are,' continues he, ' a fierce, head-ftrong, and warlike nation, and never to be reduced

reduced by force, except they are quite deftroyed, which the fituation of their country renders almoft impraddicable : befides,
obftinate fpirits are fooner to be gained by
gentle than violent meafures *. Upon this
hint Mr. Pitt improved with great advantage; and accordingly gained on them by
his wifdom, and fuperior fkill, in his appli-
cation of lenient meafures, to reconcile them
by proper and confiftent incitements: for,
it is well known, that that great man, who
knew men and manners well, inftead of
ufing thefe people by a fupercilious contempt, and diftant negledt, tempted them
with high offers of preferment, and pointed out the way to honour, both in church
and ftate, as their refpedtive worth and merit entitled them, after they had placed
themfelves under the royal ftandard.

Accordingly, this kind and prudent
ftep had the defired effedt ; and on trial
that ftatefman was enabled to declare pub-

* Chap. vi. p. 68.

lickly

lickly with patriotic boldnefs: ' I fought
for merit, and in the north I found it.'
So true was this faying, that the brave general Wolfe, and others, wifely placed no
lefs confidence in their faithfulnefs, than
fecurity in their unfhaken firmnefs and
courage, when fighting againft the enemies
of their king and country in the plains of
Montreal, when led on to the attack of
Quebec, in the American war immediately
before the laft.

A gentleman from thence remarks in his
letter to a friend, and launches out in praife
of the highlanders, in words to this purpofe:
' How proud would you be of the Britifh
nation, did you but fee the bravery of the
highlanders in their attack on Quebec, and
with what formidable rapidity they rufhed
forward into action! My God! thefe un-
daunted breechlefs fellows made the very
walls of the city tremble and fall before
them! Methinks I fee the French fly by
hundreds at the very fight of a plaid. It is
to be hoped that government will reward
thofe brave heroes who are the bulwark of
the

the nation, as well as the pride of their king and country.'

This inftance is but a faint account of their general fpirit. Let us now look out for a particular one : and the inftance that ftarts to my eye happened at the attack of Nieuport, as mentioned in the public papers of the 6th of November laft, and told as follows : ' We are happy in recording an inftance of heroifm in a common foldier belonging to the 53d regiment, in the late attack at Nieuport ; when the French preffed forward, he received a wound in his left arm ; he faid it was not worth the notice ; foon after, a mufquet-ball was lodged in his thigh ; he received another in his leg ; yet ftill he refufed to retire, faying, he would never defert his brave comrades as long as he could draw a trigger. In a fhort time after, he received a fourth ball, which went throw his head.' The name of this brave man was Duncan M'Lean, a Scotch highlander. Methinks that even this inftance will make Mr. P. blufh, unlefs his face is fteeled againft fhame.—

Here

Here is true bravery, and common to moft of the highlanders, who value themfelves lefs than their honour, a quality they are well known to keep fight of, in the hour of caufe, &c.

Much older than the above period we hear of the bravery of the Scottifh nation. The Englifh hiftorians record, that, after the Scots had gained a victory at Bannockburn, over ten times their own number, being only 30,000 ftrong, in the year 1314, they ftruck fuch terror among the enemies, that Thomas Walfingham frankly owns how the Englifh, or as Mr. Echard is pleafed to tranflate him, the unhappy borderers became fo difheartened, that a hundred of them would fly from three Scotch foldiers.

But in defiance to facts and experience, this common adverfary (as if under pay) has worked his whole wrath againft the hardy inhabitants of the mountains, without any regard to rank, diftinction, or merit; and has laboured to cover them all over with fuch an infamous garb, as his own malevolence alone could manufacture, confequently

by

by no means befitting thefe generous, brave,
and hofpitable people.

Mr. P. fpeaking of the antiquity of the
Piꝯs, remarks ' that fingle ereꝯt 'ftones are
' fepulchral memorials, or boundaries; there
' is no authority,' continues he, ' and no rea-
' fon to believe that the Celts ever ufed to
' raife hillocks over their illuftrious dead.
' The plain *Cromleachd*, or little heaps of
' ftones, were more convenient to their fa-
' vage indolence.'

The *Shians* (*i. e.* Dunipacis) or mute
hills, were fure enough raifed before the
Romans entered among them.

And it is clear, from the fpeech of Galgacus, that their manners, in thefe days,
were no lefs refined than that of the Romans, who were rude enough to call them
barbarians in common with all other nations, who would not fubmit to thefe ty-
rannical people. Therefore, unlefs Mr. P.
condefcends on the time when, and the
place where, the people whom he calls favages were in that ftate (as at prefent they
are not fo), we muft tell our readers, that
the

the epithet offered by P. proceeds from a heart overflowing with malice, and such as the Englifh language has not epithets of reproach fufficiently ftrong to exprefs our abhorrence at fuch men who are capable of infulting the public ear with fo much infamy; are therefore unworthy of notice.

But, as ufual, we muft remark his ignorance of the Celtic tongue; when he calls *Cromleac*, a little heap of ftones, whereas the *Cromleach* is a large flag laid horrizontally, not indeed always over a grave, as will be feen anon, but ufed for an altar, as the name declares.

There are erect ftones ufed at burials, as certain marks of diftinction, and thofe are to be met with every where; particularly at Barvas in Lewis, there is a ftone named *Clachntruifeal*, feventeen feet erected above the ground, and fix feet under the earth, and faftened ftrongly by other ftones at the bottom to make it firm. And Mr. P. is afked, what are the *Torrs* and *Nods*, or *Nads*, but burrying-hills? *He chean fo nod*, his head is under the fod, or in the earth.

earth. The other hillocks are to be met
with in a hundred places; and a man's going to the *Torr*, is equivalent to a man's
going to a burial; and this is indeed the
common manner of fpeaking on thefe occafions over all the north-weft of Scotland.

But to return to the *Cromleachd*, better
reading *Crow leachd cow*, altars, or flags;
when fpelt Cromleachd, the ignorant readers miftake it for bowed flag, whereas in
Gaelic the *mb* founds as *v* in Englifh;
that letter is wanting in Gaelic, *e.g. (Cromb-
leach)* Crovleachd; and this hits exactly the
idea that Toland had concerning it. ‘ *Cromleachd*,’ fays he, ‘ were large altars, or cow
altars, on which cows and oxen were facrificed; by them lies a great ftone by way
of pedeftal for fome divinity, perhaps for
Jupiter, (or idol *Crom chruach*.’)

There is a *Cromleachd* in Navern parifh, in Pembrokefhire, ftill eighteen feet
high; and nine broad; and by it lies a piece
broken off ten feet long, more than twenty
oxen could draw *.

* Toland's Collection of feveral things. Mufeum.

The

The fituation which is generally chofen for the *Cromleachs* is judicious, and nothing is more exact than the plains of fome of them; which fhew that thofe who erected them were very folicitous to place them as confpicuous as poffible. Sometime this flat ftone, and its fupporters, ftand upon the plain natural foil and common level of the ground; and at other times, it is placed on the fummit of a barrow made either of ftone or earth. It is fometimes placed in the middle of a circle of ftones; and when it has a place of that dignity, muft be fuppofed to be erected on fome extraordinary occafion. It is more generally placed on the edge of the circle, efpecially if there is a ftone erected in the middle of the circle, as may be feen near Callarifh, in Lewis. There are many of them in Cornwall; and from their rude fimplicity they feem to be Druid-ical monuments; a ftrong proof that the order of Druids is of old ftanding. The fields on which they ftand in Ireland are cal-led *magh fleachd*, that is, fields of worfhip; and they derive their authorities from their

being

being worſhipping in the plains (of *magh*
ſleachd) the very day that the *Tighernmas,*
king of Ireland, and firſt author of idolatry,
died in the 3034 year of the world, when they
were ſacrificing to *Cromh Cruach.* No nation can come up to the Iriſh in point of
exact chronologies, but their authorities are
diſcredited in many particulars, and juſtly.

This accurate piece of Iriſh intelligence
is further coroborated by Tolland's giving
an account of *Cromh Cruach,* which, he ſays,
is a heap of crooked ſtones in their natural
ſtate. That being the moſt famous idol of
Ireland, it ſtood in the middle of 12 obeliſks
on a hill in Brigtin, in the county of Cavan.
It is ſaid to have been covered with gold and
ſilver, (a ſingular account of one ſtone; but
paſſing this,) quere, whether is not the
Cromh Cruaich, i. e. the creator of cows,
the name given to this grand idol, the ſame
with the creator of heaven and earth, alſo
meant under this ſymbol, and a proof that
the Druids firſt worſhipped the only living,
and true god ?

L   Borlaiſe,

Borlaife, however, maintains that the *Cromh leachd* were not altars, and adduces feveral reafons to prove them to be fepulchral monuments, becaufe fome of them are 17 feet high, others not large, nor flat enough for facrificing upon them, and of courfe he he is decidedly of the opinion that they were the *Kift vaine* (or rather *Kift bharu*, dead coffins) being an area of about the fize of the body, enclofed by fide ftones pitched on end, without any covering ftone, except the large flat *cromleachd* on the top.

Befides, the *Cromh leachd*, adds he, is often furrounded with barrows, where moft of the dead were anciently buried, and no fmall reafon to think that the *Cromleachd* was fet apart for the more honourable dead.

But this far fetched reafoning, however plaufible, does not deftroy the probability of fome of the more low, and large ones being ufed for cow altars, thofe within circles e-fpecially, as obferved above ; thofe ftones erected on high pillars may, indeed, have been made covers for their great princes, and heroes, as at prefent we fee many fuch in church-

church-yards which certainly were not called *Crov leachds,* or cow altars originally ;.
becaufe the true Gealic names of fuch mean
Crudh leachds, image ftones, viz. grave-
ftones, with images of armed men en-
graved upon them, as *Crudh* fignifies an
image or figure ; and many fuch are to be
feen at Weftminifter, and in moft ancient
churches and chapels where perfonages of
rank have been interred : and there are few
church-yards over all Britain and the ifles,
where fuch are not to be feen in great plenty, moft of which are raifed high, either
upon pillars, or other buildings for the purpofe of preferving them from finking in earth,
or from being broken by accidents ; to preferve the memory of their friends from oblivion as long as poffible, and to perpetuate
from generation to generation the antiquites
of families in the bounds where thefe and
fuch monuments are, or were raifed.

Thus we may juftly obferve no wife man
will attempt to entertain the world in a language of which he himfelf is no competent
judge. One truely feels for Mr. P. and
is at a lofs whether to pronounce him

an object of pity or contempt for ex-
poling himfelf fo unguardedly to the fevere lafh of the injured.

Mr.Martin, indeed, on whofe authority he
fometimes depends, has given a very juft defcription of one of the temples in Liewes,
though it is fince much hurt by a neighbouring Goth, who has dragged the ftones from
it to make lintels and other ufes for new
houfes he is building. And it is to be
hoped, that Mr. M'Kenzie ~~~~ put a
ftop to fuch facrilege for the honour of his
country.

Dr. Macperfon fays, the circles of ftones
fo often mentioned by Offian, and fo frequent in the north Ebudes, were the work
of the *Pictifh Druids*; and though fimple in
their conftruction, are not unworthy of the
curious ; they were the temples where the
priefts employed by our anceftors, in the
fervice of their idols, perfomed the moft folemn offices of their fuperftition. Still the
people agree in calling the circles holy places, and fometimes holy temples, nor will
they in general allow the leaft ftone in thefe
temples to be touched, left they fhould dif-
turb

turb the genius of the place; however there is no general rule without fome exceptions; and in Callarnifh we meet with one of thefe.

The Druids, as priefts dedicated to the facred office of religion, muft have had temples; as men, they muft have had houfes, for the habitations of the better fort; as they were abfolute judges in every cafe of importance, they had their forums, or feperate courts of judicature; as the firft clafs of nobility they were certainly buried, efpecially the chief Flamins, with fome diftinction, and confequently muft have had fepulchres, the moft remarkable, which the time they lived in afforded.

Now as all thefe things were intended for the ufe of pofterity, as well as the age that erected them; it is no wonder that many of them have furvived the fate of their fuperftition; but as the country improved and became more cultivated, many of thefe ancient monuments were doubtlefs applied to other ufes as building, for which reafon few of them are now to be feen near great cities and towns. However, in the rocky

L 3   hilly

hilly countries, and retired places, fuch as the highlands and ifles of Britain, many of them are ftill remaining.

The Druids and other great perfonages unqueftionably built their apartments, it is very reafonable to fuppofe, and their principal priefts and great men had grave ftone vaults (*Kift vane*) placed in them, fays Borlaife, where the afhes were collected, either near fome place of worfhip, or adjoining their dwelling houfes, without any other note of diftinction or rank; and fometimes they built barrows over their urns; as thefe are to be met with almoft in every country; this accounts for the Cairns, mentioned by Dr. Mac Pherfon, having burnt bones and afhes in the urns; and yet the Cairns are not applied to the ufe of fepulchres folely, but to other purpofes alfo, as refidence for families to fecure them from the inclemency of the feafon in thefe cold countries, with a kind of little burying chapel within, or clofely adjoining to them; and their keeping urns in their dwelling houfes, with the relicts of their friends, are neither more ftriking, nor impolitical in the Druids, than in Chriftians

keep-

keeping arms, teeth, and other relicts in more modern times by way of refpect, and other pretended ufeful purpofes, as is well known to have been the cafe in their palaces and inferior houfes over all Europe; is to the Chriftians even yet.

But the Dr.'s, I mean Mr. Martin's, authority in many things, on account of his extreme credulity and his unbounded curiofity, fhould be carefully examined before his whole account of the ifles fhould be adopted as of undoubted authenticity.

Who can believe his narrative of the Scheanachies fhutting their doors and windows for the fpace of a day, with a large ftone lying on their bellies, and their heads covered about with their plaids, pumping up their brains for rhetorical encomiums, embellifhed by Mr. P.; for, without fuch unnatural exertions, even at this day the bards and common people in thefe ifles will make encomiums and fatires extempore, tho' not their daily profeffion. How much more could a learned, able, and experienced bard,

one fet apart on purpofe on account of his
fuperior abilities be able to entertain his au-
dience, without throwing himfelf into the
ridiculous and diftreffing attitude, in which
he is reprefented before his powers of poetry
could be exerted.

We cannot believe that he faw the grave
in the chapel of Sanda in the Orkneys, 19
feet long, with the large back bone; nor
the large lunar ftone at Scalpay, that advanced and retired according to the increafe or
decreafe of the moon; the author avers this
to be falfe from his own knowledge, having
refided for years on that ifle and neither faw
nor heard of fuch a miracle, much lefs of
the ftrange prodigy at Rowdle, nor the ftory
of the feals and ravens, which never was believed : the fingular oddity at Rowdle, called
St. Clement's blind man, is faid to have loft
his fight for two days at every change of the
moon; nor the regular coupling of feals, and
their fagacity at finding out the brute that
would venture to take advantage of the fe-
male, in the abfence of her mate with his
terrible revenge by leaving the fea red with
the

the blood of the aggreffor, and that the feals made their addreffes to each other by kiffes; indeed the natural (not artificial) cave of *Ullard*, and two wells in it, where one man might defend himfelf againft a thoufand, as it has a perpendicular rock of 20 fathoms immediately before the mouth of this cave, which is truely natural, is fact, and the only part of the narrative that may be depended on.

It is to be feen near the fummit of a high hill, called *Ully-bheal* in *Harris*; nay, *Tolland* alfo has been impofed on refpecting the two ravens at Valay, and other two in Berneray, and as many in Troda to keep thefe ifles clear of more of thefe carnivorous birds, and the eagles in Liewis that were poffeffed of fagacity enough to keep their own country free from damage.

Read, to the contrary, Lanne B.'s Travels in the Ebudæ, and there it will appear that all thefe places are infefted with thoufands of thefe birds; that M'Kenzie in particular gives half a crown for each of their heads, to any of the inhabitants who kills an eagle or raven; and the above humourfome things were the

grofs

grofs impofitions of the accute, but farcaf-
tic inhabitants, who wanted to fatiate this
uncommonly curious gentleman with ro-
mantick farces of their own fertile imagina-
tions, which the unwary Dr. believed for
truths, and vended them to others for facts
and Mr. P. lays hold of this gentleman's authority when it anfwers his purpofe of ridicule, or wants to miflead his reader; but
few of them, it is faid, believe Mr. P's
account, as his violence has damned his
works, and difappointed his hopes of fuc-
cefs; fo that his own words may be repeated to him, as he did to the Macpherfons; tho' ready to vent improper authori-
zed falfehood, and lyes, there is no danger
from them; for as folly is the caufe of villa-
ny, fo alfo of detection.

‘ Our poor Scots antiquifts are enemies to
‘ the Piks,’ adds Mr. P.; ‘ it is their trade to
‘ fight againft authorities, truth, and com-
‘ mon fenfe; on this occafion being ignorant
‘ of the grand features of our hiftory, that
‘ the *Piks* were a Gothic people, they have
‘ blundered

' blundered in utter darknefs, and had re-
' courfe to abfurd ingenuity.'

Mr. P. is not aware that reafon, and not
railing, generally convince the fenfible reader; and with this we leave his Gothic Piks to
his own management, until fomething like
reafon is advanced by him to enforce his argument, and fhall follow him to the Ebudæ,
a place well known to the author, though
not to Mr. P.

' Anno 240, Solinus wrote that the 5 Ebu-
' dæ ifles are feparated by narrow channels,
' (this is an undoubted fact) but when he
' mentions *Rum, Skye,* and *Tyrie* among
' thefe,' he betrays great ignorance of the
country, for fome of thefe ifles are 70, or
80 miles from the Ebudæ, and the neareft
of them 24 computed, or 36 Englifh miles
diftant. Mr. P. affirms, ' that Richard
' means the fame thing in his defcription of
them, viz. *Liewis, N. and S. Uift, Coll,
Tyrie, and Skye;* this fpecimen may point
out how cautious people ought to be in truft-
ing to mifinformed authors, when even
thefe geographers are fo wide of the truth.

The

The five real Ebudæ are *Liewis*, and *Harris*, the two *Uifls* and *Barray*.

Thefe are divided by fmall channels of eight miles acrofs each of them. There are four iflands in Uift, twelve hours out of 24 each day; as Valay, North Uift, Benbecula, and South Uift, and the other twelve hours the country is one continued fpace of *terra firma* where horfe and foot paffengers travel on dry land. Three large fheets of fea cover the channels during the flux, and full tide, that any veffel might fail over each, and at ebb-tide the hard bed of fand becomes a pleafant paffage for horfe or foot paffengers.

‘ A native of Iceland, Mr. *Thowrclin*, pro-
‘ feffor of hiftory, informs me,’ contiues Mr.
P. ‘ that the very date of erecting thefe cir-
‘ cular monuments, meaning the Druidical
‘ temples, and their ufes, is contained in
‘ the annals of the old laws of the country;
‘ as well as their names in popular mouths,
‘ namely Ting, a court.

Tacitus mentions groves, it is true, but thefe were ufed to burn the facrifices, where
peats

peats were not convenient. The *Druids*,
according to Borlaife and moft other authors, chofe groves to worfhip in, as the
Canaanites did. ' The *Druids*,' fays he,
' though the ftricteft of all fects, carried it
into excefs, performing their facred rites,
not in houfes, but under confecrated oaks.'
No generally received opinion is more
falfely founded, than that the *Druids* retired
under groves and fecret receffes to worfhip
their divinities. The very reverfe is appa-
rently the fact over all Britain, and Scotland in particular; becaufe there, inftead of
groves, the *Druids* pitched their temples in
the plaineft open flat fields, where wood
could not grow for want of foil; and in
the ifland of Liewis, the grand arched Druidical temple, and all others around it, are
planted on plain deep mofs, and each of
them enclofed with a circular funk fence,
ftill vifible, cut around them, to keep off
cattle from treading on the hallowed
ground; and all this behoved to be done
long after the woods were fallen, as the
                                          ftone

ftone pillars are funk fix feet deep in the mofs, and thefe firmly .fupported by ftones.

The Greeks, with their foolifh Drus, *quercus*, fignifying oak, believed that to be the name, in fpite of the real *Gaelic* word, *Tru* or *Truo*, a fervant or fupplicant of the Divinity, and known ftill by that name in the Chriftian worfhip ; and the Divinity is commonly addreffed by *Peccarin Truo*, or finful fervant or fervants. By thus un-guardedly depending on the Greeks and Romans, moft hiftorians have been mifled ; which would not have been the cafe had they relied on the inhabitants in their dif-ficulties about etymologies here, and on many other occafions.

But Strabo is perfectly clear on the head. According to him, *Drus* is not a word of Greek extraction; the Greeks being thought too modern in comparifon to the *Druids*, who were famous from the moft remote antiquity, long before Greece could boaft of their wife men and philofophers ; who were really beholden to the Druids, and co-
.   pied

pied them in many particulars; while the
Druids are allowed to be as old as the mi-
gration of the Celts from the Eaſt; long
before the Greeks were heard of.

It is not on that account probable, ſays
Borlaiſe, that they would borrow their
name from a nation which they ſo much
ſurpaſſed in antiquity. Alexander Poly-
hiſtor, in Clemens Alexandrinus, maintains,
that even *Pythagoras* heard both the *Druids* and *Brachmans* in their reſpective countries; and we can ſcarce imagine that ſo
curious a traveller as *Pythagoras* could be
induced to traverſe almoſt all the then
known world in order to converſe with
them, and examine the principles upon
which they proceeded in ſearch of wiſdom,
by any thing leſs than becauſe both the
Druids and *Brachmans* made at that time a
conſiderable figure in their diſcourſes and
WRITINGS. This man travelled to *Aſia*,
Egypt, and the *Weſt*, and it is thought that
Pythagoras borrowed the *metempſichoſis*, or
tranſmigration of ſouls from the *Druids*, as
remarked by Friek, p. 38. I know of au-
thers

thors who contend that the *Druids* borrowed this tenet from *Pythagoras.* At any
rate, the intimacy between *Abaris* and *Pythagoras* was confiderable ; and the Greeks
had little learning before *Pythagoras*, as is
well known. Thefe miftakes of authors,
refpecting *Drus*, had been cleared up in
many other parts, as well as at Callarnifh, over thofe ifles, were they inquifitive in their enquiries. Temples are
built in places there where wood could
not grow owing to the nature of the foil,
being over-run with fhelly fand, which naturally deftroys the young fprigs and roots
of trees ; and Mr. B—n never met with a
circle either in the middle, or even fkirt of
a wood, but uniformly on plains, removed
from the copfe. Indeed common fenfe,
with a little reflection from the reader, is on
his fide, feeing the *Druids* had the power of
life and death in their hands, being terrors
to evil doers, and a praife, as well as protection, to fuch as did well ; fo they required
no places of concealment for themfelves,
but they appeared openly, to be feen by the
people, that they might at times be eye and

ear-

ear-witneffes to the principles and practices of the natives, over whom they had unlimited authority, and paffed fentence according to their good or bad behaviour. I muft confefs indeed with Borlaife, that if we take only a fuperficial view of the *Druid* fuperftition, without examining the hiftory of other countries, we fhall be apt to think that the *Druids* ftand alone in all the inftances of barbarity, magic, grove worfhip ; and their human facrifices fhock us. Their magic belief, with their oak worfhip, looks fingular and abfurd ; but the moft diftinguifhed part of their *Druidical* fuperftition, their grove worfhip, was common to them, with the *Jews*, and the *Canaanites*, who facrificed human victims, as did many other favage people, to appeafe fome imaginary enraged Divinity ; to whom nothing was thought more grateful.

One of the reafons why the *Druids* were fuppofed to be fond of grove worfhip, was on account of the *mifletoe* which grew on the oak, to which they paid a kind of divine worfhip. Even in this they were not

M   fingular,

fingular, for the *Perfians* and *Maffagete*, thought the *mifletoe* divine. Virgil tells us, that EVANDER was facrificing in his grove, without the city, when Æneas came to him.

Yet all inftances that are given do not prove that regular circles were ever built in groves, but only a conjecture that it is likely they might have facrificed in their groves on certain folemn occafions, when their *holocauft* required much fire-wood; which was more conveniently had in their groves, and with much lefs trouble and ex- pence, than to carry great quantities to the more open fields, where their regular tem- ples generally ftood.

In after times, when the Greeks became a polifhed nation, the Gauls had a fchool at Marfeilles; and thefe people became very fond of every thing that was Grecian ; for in Cæfar's time writings were found in the camp of the Helvetij, relating to their dif- ferent orders, and all wrote in Greek cha- racters. From this time all the *Druids* underftood the Greek tongue, and the moft learned of them did occafionally ufe it. Nay, the

the Irifh *Druids* had their form of letters
called their *Beth-luis-nion*, in which every
letter, to the number of twenty-fix, was
called after fome tree of the wood.

So much for Druidifm.

It is not difputed but that may be the
cafe with regard to the above Ting of Shetland, Norway, and Denmark ; but it is denied to agree, except in part, to the *Druidi-*
cal temples in Scotland, and in the ifles particularly ; for I alfo converfed with Mr.
Thoroclin on the very fpot where the
four grand Druidical temples of the ancient
Hyperborians lie, and gave him all the information he called for ; and agreeable to his
requeft remitted more to Copenhagen after
him.

And on that account, to point out my
inclination to coincide with Mr. Pinkerton
in whatever appears rational, it is granted,
that thefe grand circular temples may, with
propriety enough, have been frequently ufed
on folemn occafions by their kings and fupreme judges, as courts for difcuffing very
weighty matters relative to the government

of

of the ftates, and yet neverthelefs be ufed
as temples for inftructing their congrega-
tions at the ftated times fet apart for religious worfhip.   This being a practice
handed down by them to pofterity, as the
fame is manifeft from the records of ancient times, when churches have been employed by Chriftian kings, or the like, or
fome fuch, when great national affemblies
meet.   And thefe are alfo the fentiments
of Mr. James Anderfon when writing from
the ftate papers in king Robert the Bruce's
time.

‘ It may not be amifs,’ fays he, ‘ to obferve, that the places of parliament's
meeting in thofe ancient times were ufually in fome noted churches ; and the acts
paffed, had not only the king's feal append-
ed to them, but alfo the feals of the chief
prelates and nobles, who, for themfelves and
their fucceffors, fwore upon the evangelifts,
to the true obfervation of thefe acts ; and the
reft of the parliament, with uplifted hands,
before the altar, promifed the like.’   Now,
as this ancient practice of holding parlia-

ments extended much farther back than the
thirteenth century, there is no improprie-
t. in fuppofing, that the *Druids*, the kings
and nobles of their time, had fet the example to their defcendants, and made the
circles, in proportion to their grandeur, anfwer the fame double capacity of holding
grand affemblies, and alfo inferior courts
of juftice as the nature of the times and
circumftances required, and at the fame
time continued them as ftated places of
worfhip when the people ufually affembled
for religious inftruction from their priefts.
And as the Chriftian people have alfo other
places for holding courts, befide their
churches, which are feldom now ufed, except on fome extraordinary cafes for fecu-
cular bufinefs; fo alfo had the *Druids* their
Shians, or mute-hills, called *Mars-hills*; in
Gaelic, *Tomm amhoid*; and the court-hills,
Lagh-dun, i. e. law-hill, near Perth, to
collect their fubjects in order to hear and
determine their feveral differences according
to the pleadings on both fides; and the
judges pronounced fentence from the apex

M 3   of

of thefe artificial hills, or *Duns*, which were heard with attention by the people who ftood on the fides of thefe eminences below the chief fpeaker, or *Fergu*, and executed it accordingly.

Nor could Mr. Thoroclin, when there, make more of thefe circles than other people, who, without difparagement, are no lefs knowing to form a juft opinion of the circles than he was, being natives of the country, namely, to allow them to be named *Team-ple nan Druiy*, the temple of the Druids; nor did Mr. Thoroclin know a word of the language, except the few names already mentioned, and thefe are well known by the moft illiterate native to be of Norwegian extraction, before his arrival, and after his departure from thence; and my afferting this fact ought to gain more credit, than the ignorant affirmation of a gentleman to the contrary, who knows neither the country nor language.

The people of Liewis are equally affected at the Druidical temples, as Mr. Bofwell was at the ruins of Icolmkill; while con-

con-

templating the venerable ruins, he reflected
with much fatisfaction that the folemn
fcenes of piety never lofe their fanction and
influence, though the cares and follies may
prevent us from vifiting them, and may
even make us fancy that their effects are only as yefterday when it is paft; fo in the fame
manner, the very fight of thefe venerable
circles will ftrike a ftranger with reverence
that, accompanied with the traditionary
accounts of their fanctity, command the refpect of the natives for them; and there are
many hills in that place raifed long ago, for
the exprefs purpofe of holding courts of juftice upon, independant of the religious circles, as their names fufficiently indicate, to
fatisfy any reafonable fearcher after antiquities.

   ' Mr. Pinkerton maintains that there
' were no faints among the Picts, but
' Welch or Irifh church-men, before the
' eleventh century, and that Galloway was
' unknown till then.'

   This man if he can, will leave them nothing that is valuable, but HIMSELF;

           a very

a very honourable acquifition, fure e-
nough !

We muft however, put him in mind that
St. Gildas, *St. Martin, St, Ninian*, bifhop
of Whitburn in Galloway, though not
known before the eleventh century, accor-
cing to P. *St. Patrick Cumineus* and *Ada-
manan, St. Machua* of Kilmahog, and *St.
Fillan*. Both thefe laft were in Perthfhire ;
all of them, and many more than can be
mentioned, were not only Scots and Piéts,
but flourifhed moft of them before the 8th
century. St. Machua, bifhop of Kilmahog,
lived anno 700 ; and the wells named after
him are efteemed very falutary for purging
the human body of extraneous foreign hu-
mours, that are obnoxious to a found mind,
conftitution, and policy.

But they are not to be compared to the
waters of Strathfillan, which that St. hath
impregnated with the bleffing of curing lu-
nacy. This good Saint flourifhed anno 703;
and, according to Heétor Boethius and T.
Dempfter, was not only a Saint, but a bifhop
and abbot, viz. bifhop of Fife, and had a
strong

ftrong caftle in Lochlevin, and abbot of Argylefhire, or at Strathfillan, by the very Dorfum of Alabin, where the famous wells were, and are vifited yearly by deranged people of every rank : even fmatterers in learning have returned from thence perfectly purged of malice, and rancour, and cured with imaginary found health. Thefe waters are vifited even from Edinburgh, and 60 miles around by lunatics.

‘ When the patient,’ fays T. Dempfter, ‘ is wafhed in the water of Strathfillan, and put to fleep in the Saint’s bed in the old temple, bound, at night ; if the patient is found unbound in the morning, it is reckoned a good omen, and propitious ; but if not un-tied, he is pronounced incurable.’

The arm of this Saint was a precious re-lict, preferved by the king of the Picts, and afterwards of the Scots, in the caftle of Dun-fermline, locked up in a filver box, and was carried by holy Mauritius, abbot of Inch-peffray, at the battle of Bannochburn, and to it the victory is afcribed, as appears from Boethius.

St.

*St. Fillanus episcopus et abbas sanctissimæ
recordationis apud nostrates florebat in Fifa
et Argadie cui templum & arx munitissima
in Laco Levinio habebat* *.

*Rex Robertus Brussius, cum precibus per-
severaverit, capsula argentea sponte, nullo
tangente aperta, verum Bracchium quod domi
relictum, sacerdoti ostendit quo rex et milites
armati præclaram victoriam attinebant* †.

And one of the Saint's teeth, with an ivo-
ry fword, is ſtill preſerved with the greateſt care at the caſtle of Lanne as a famous
relict; both in proof of the antiquity of that
ancient family of Lanne, and of their connection with this Saint; and theſe people
are known to be among the old inhabitants
of the Pictiſh nation; and for any thing
known to the contrary, might have once
ranked among the kings of theſe people: And
how does Mr. P. know but this fword was
the ſpiritual weapon of warfare uſed by this
good old ecclefiaſtic, and might alſo have

* Hect. Boet.
† Thomas Dempſter, 1627.

been

been brandished against the enemy along
with this famous arm, and stretched out by
the above holy abbot, on that memorable
day, when three hundred thousand are
known to have been totally routed; and
moreover the tooth also might be presented
that day *in terrorem?* To fall under one's
teeth is disagreeable, but to fall under such a
tooth as St. Fillan's is terror complete. It is
of course rather dangerous for Mr. P. to deny his being a Pictish bishop so boldly, especially as the effects of his goodness are yearly experienced by those who apply to him;
so, if too much provoked by an adversary the
force of his wrath may prove no less terrible, if felt by such as are offensive to him.

His medicinal waters at Strathfillan in
Perthshire are also much used for distem-
pered cattle; and such as have not always
the benefit of using it on the spot; generally
carry home large pieces of leaven, which
they prepare at the wells; and when any
malady seizes on their horses, cows, or sheep,
they are not only washed, but made to drink
the waters of this leaven at home, to restore
them

them to their health again. So much for Pictish bishops; and many more can be mentioned, if neceffary.

Now, as Mr. P. did not know this be-fore, he is forgiven; only let him not pre-tend ignorance in future, as thefe facts are too well attefted, to be difputed. More *Pictifh* Saints can be mentioned, if thefe are not fufficient to eftablifh the real exif-tence of Caledonian Saints who were born among thefe people, which were neither Welch nor Irifh, as that expreffion is at prefent underftood, tho' no real highlander acknowledges the term Ireland to belong to Scotland, nor to the Gaelic fpoken there.

' Ay,' but adds Mr. P. ' Englifh was a
' written language, while there is no reafon
' to fuppofe the *Pictifh* was ever committed
' to parchment, in a rude, and barbarous
' kingdom, while the *Belgic* and Englifh
' had been long the written language of a
' civilized nation.'

This gentleman returns again and again to the charge, and forces his antagonift to have recourfe to almoft the fame dull round

of

of argument to beat him out of his hold.
However difagreeable this mode muft be to
the reader, let us with patience hear
what Innis fays on this head ; ' it is a wonder,' fays he, ' that we have any remains
of MSS. occafioned, firft, by cafual accidents ; fecondly, by being plundered of
them, or deftroyed on purpofe by a powerful enemy, Edward the firft ; and thirdly,
by the zeal of Knox, and the violent refor-
mers, who burnt all the noble edifices, and
papers contained in them: this is accounting
for the want of written manufcripts in Scotland, though it is beyond doubt that fuch
exifted there, and I add that long prior to
thefe times, the moft valuable of the *Pic-
tijh* writings were deftroyed by KENNETH
MAC ALPIN, and his Scots, when they
overturned the Caledonian kingdom in the
ninth century, and particularly the famous
metropolis of Camelodunum, of that kingdom, which for the obftinate and long refiftance made by the inhabitants againft that
aggreffor, was not only burnt and erafed to
the ground with papers, and all other valu-
ble

ble articles contained in it; but the whole inhabitants, man, woman, and child were put to the fword. In this mercilefs maffacre the whole valuable records of Britain were annihilated; and if Mr. P. doubts this fact, we can confront him with authority in fupport of the affertion.

This total deftruction of Camelodunum, with all its inhabitants, has miflead not only Boethius, but many of his followers, particularly John Lefsly, bifhop of Rofs, into the full belief that the whole nation of the *Picts* were deftroyed by Kenneth Mac Alpin; becaufe, fays he, againft the law obferved by all nations, they flew the ambaffadors fent them; (reflecting no doubt on the treatment, he himfelf met with when in that kind of capacity and fent by Queen Mary to act at the Englifh court, for her intereft, and was imprifoned in the Tower of London for a fpace, and even condemned, tho' by the interceffion of the king of France he efcaped with his life;) ' on that accout,' fays he, ' Kenneth as king of the Scots who fent to the Picts to demand the kingdom of their land,

land, which by juft fucceffion pertained to
him, and on refufal and treachery extermi-
nated, the whole nation;' than which nothing is more contrary to truth, and to the
wifdom of that king; even if he had been
able, which does not appear to have been
the cafe, from the ftrength, and great
numbers of the Picts; for they increafed fo
faft, as Gouch remarks, that the foil could
neither maintain, nor hold them, on which
account they were obliged to invade, and
overrun the Roman provinces; and Stillingfleet imagines that the South Britons were
willing to make room for the Picts, for the
fake of peace, by yeilding up the whole
country between the two walls for their colonies, when the Romans could no longer
keep them under fubjection, on the retreat
of Severus, with the lofs of fifty-two thoufand men.

Yet Mr. Innis, who is otherwife favourable to the Picts, laments that both their name
and language difappeared, and ceafed in the
middle of the twelfth century, and that
Gaelic fucceeded to it; he however makes an

apology

apology for his ignorance of that language, to decide dogmatically on that head, and his apology is accepted of. Henry Huntington, an Englifh hiftorian, who wrote about the middle of the 12th century, feemed to believe alfo that the language of the *Picts* was then extinct; but being no judge of the tongue, he alfo is an incompetent one to determine the fate of that language. Richard of Hex-am however writes that, at the battle of Stan-dard, *anno domini* 1138, David king of the Scots was forced to give to the Picts the right hand, as their right on that day; a proof that neither the people, nor language were extinct, but on the contrary were a very powerful hoft; fo that the total deftruction of a nation far more powerful than the Scots is highly improbable. It is allowed that many of their princes and leaders fuffered, and that moft of their powerful princes, con-nected with the ancient royal family, were removed, and obliged to fly to diftant re-mote parts of the kingdom, and their pla-ces were fupplied by the relations of the conqueror to ftrengthen his hand; and alfo, that

that the metropolis met with the deftruction
, already defcribed for their refiftance, and
breach of promife, but the reft of the lower clafs, and fuch of the nobility as fubmit-
ted, were moft certainly taken under protection.

Nay, as a proof of the falfenefs of fo impolitical and cruel an action as the total ex-
tirpation of a whole nation, Nennius tells
us, that Kenneth Mac Alpin was called king
of the Picts, as were alfo his fucceffors, as
quoted by Lynch in the Ulfter Annals. That
the Picts made a part of the king of Albany's army in Scotland, we have plain proofs
from Ethelwood in his Chronicle *. And
Ingulphus declares, that the Picts made a
part of Conftantine king of Albany's army
at the battle of Brunford, againft *Adelftan*
king of the Saxons. In the eleventh century the *Picts* are known by their own name;
they were alfo known by the name of *Picts*
in Galloway in the twelfth century, and
other parts of the country. From the let-

* A. D. 937.

N   ter,

ter, of Rhodolph, bifhop of Canterbury, to
Pope Calixtus 1122, it appears that the Piĉts
of Galloway, and the Piĉts of Murray affected a kind of independency, and were very
troublefome under Malcolm the Fourth, being uneafy under the Scots kings, till the
king, partly by force, and partly by confent, was obliged to difperfe them through
different parts of the kingdom; thofe of
Murray were fent fouth, as the Murrays
and Douglaffes, and thofe of the fouth, were
fent north to fill their places *.

  Thus we join iffue with Innis in allowing
that the leading men who would not fubmit
to Kenneth retired partly to Galloway, and
partly to Murray and Sutherland, as to the
two extremities of the kingdom, and were not
fo eafily brought under fubjeĉtion, as many
of the lower order, to fubmit to the Scottifh
government; but muft differ with Innis re-
fpeĉting the language of the Piĉts, which
I maintain to be the fame now in the

* Anno 1159, Chronicon Pafleti, M. S. Biblioth.
Reg. Lond.

mouths

mouths of the posterity of the *Picts* as it
was in Kenneth MacAlpin's time, and long
prior to that date, as already fully made
good in the preceding part of the account
given of the name PEICH.

And as it is a severe reflection upon the political prudence, honour, and
humanity of that wise king to hold him
up before the world as a monster capable of
so much barbarity against the subdued Picts,
the opposite truth in his favour cannot be
too often mentioned to wipe away the infamous stain, and convince writers of their
own mistakes in following misinformed writers so closely.

Independent of these facts, let common
sense be appealed to; and can it once be supposed the clergymen of the different monas-
teries, and other seminaries of learning in
N. Britain, were not equally learned with
others of the same standing over all Europe?
To imagine the contrary would be giving
the lie to facts, independent of tradition, as
is manifest from the numbers of learned
gentlemen, who were employed in high
stations in every kingdom and court through

all

all Europe ; and nothing but their learning could place them fo high in rank in the republick of letters, wherever they were fettled.

Certainly Mr. P. himfelf does not believe that the ufe of letters were unknown in fuch learned feminaries, as JONA, ORANSA, and ARD CHATTAN monafteries, or abbeys; alfo in the nunneries and monafteries of UIST, and ROWDLE, the deanery of Rofs, with many more of the kind in other parts of N. Britain, as they are allowed to have been through all Europe at the fame time ; were there no poffitive proofs of the facts now exifting, it would be abfurd in the extreme to refufe or deny it.

' Our monks muft have underftood the ' learned language, and they muft like- ' wife have wrote, yes, and in Gaelic too,' ' fays Mr. M'Nicol, as already remarked.'

Anno 1139, long before there was any printing in Europe, we are told by Sir Robert Sibbald, that, in a written manufcript fent to him by a gentleman of the family of Mac Intofh, he finds that the predeceffor of the Earls of Weems in Fife is called therein

EOIN

Eoin mor na Vamh, in Gaelic; that is, *Great John of the Cave.* *Uye,* a Gaelic name given to any beautiful plain field, confined, either by two feas, lochs, rivers, or mountains; as we meet with many fuch over all the ifles, as well as this Uye in Fife, or the Uye of Sir R. Menzies in Appin a Du, in Perthfhire. Here then we meet with written Gaelic even in Fife, long prior to that time mentioned by the imperious Mr. Pinkerton.

Nay, moreover, before the year 1054, we learn from Turgot, bifhop of St. Andrews, while he was preceptor to king Malcolm Kenmore's children, and who had much accefs to learn the hiftory of the royal family, that Gaelic was not only a written, but the only language generally fpoken in Scotland then, and he accordingly delineates the character of Margaret, the queen of Scotland, whom, he fays, he had often heard difcourfe on fubtile queftions of theology, in prefence of the moft learned men of the kingdom, and adds, that Malcolm the king underftood the Gaelic language, as well as the

N 3   Saxon,

Saxon ; the firft being the vernacular language of N. Britain, and taught him when
a child, before he fled to England, from
Macbeth, the ufurper of his crown, where
he learned to fpeak Englifh.

The king therefore willingly performed
the office of interpreter between his royal
confort and the Scottifh ecclefiaftics, who
were perfect mafters of the learned languages, and could tranflate them into Gaelic,
but were quite ignorant of the Englifh as far
back, as anno 1093; becaufe Gaelic was
the language even of the court, as well as of
the commoners, before the Englifh grandees
and many others of inferior rank were forced
into Scotland by William the Conqueror.
And Turgot fays, that the Gaelic clergymen
were convinced of the force of the queen's
arguments, and yielded to them, even tho'
the king's Gaelic tranflation of thefe behoved
to be much inferior in point of energy, to
the original delivered by the pious and learned queen in the Saxon, or Englifh tongue.

If Mr. P. pleafes he may examine the accounts themfelves, and they will convince
him

him of his miftaken notion of the Gaelic
and its antiquity. It is hoped he will not lofe
his temper in finding as old written parchment in Scotland, as he tells us we may meet
with in England, and in Gealic too, an almoft unknown language, though the moft
honourable remains of the antiquities of Britain, &c. and no language is more powerful
and expreffive in the mouth of a poet or
orator to this day.

But it would be entertaining to behold
Mr. P.'s countenance when he reads that
there were kings in thefe defpifed ifles, long
before the Chriftian æra, and for any thing
proved to the contrary, for centurys before
the firft Fergus is faid to have been invited
from Ireland, to head the North Britifh ar-
mies; for this laft name is only an *agnomen*
common to moft kings, both before and after
that time, and applied to them as fupreme
judges, when they paffed fentence in that
capacity in their different courts of judicature, as may perhaps more fully appear elfewhere.

N 4 But

But to return at prefent to the kings of the ifles. One of thefe fturdy aggreffors, named Bridan Mor na Hwai, or as he is named in Uift, Bridan Gop Dearag, *Bridan with the red mouth*, landed in Scotland about the Chriftian æra, with only a thoufand of his men, and was beat off; but this bold invader and progenitor of the Mac Donalds landed the year following with a more powerful army, and impudently enough fettled himfelf by force of arms in Argyle, and would neither allow the imaginary *Twa de Dannans*, the *Dalriads*, nor the Irifh Scots to fettle in thefe quarters, nor give names to any part of that country, but as he pleafed.

The account given by William Buchanan of Auchmar, who publifhed his enquiry into the genealogy, and prefent ftate of the ancient Scottifh furnames of the Irifh Scots, in the year 1723, coincides almoft with the foregoing narrative; from which we may infer the impoffibility no lefs than the improbability of their landing in Cantire; and it is as follows: In treating of the Mac Donalds, he fays, COLL, VUAIS's fon, was called

GILLEBRIED,

GILLEBRIED, or as our hiftories name him, *Bridius.* This *Bridius,* in the reign of king *Ederus,* about 54 years before our Saviour's nativity, with an army of his highlanders entered Morven, and the other weftern continent, which having, with great barbarity depopulated, he was in his return met by king *Ederus* with an army, and entirely defeated; BRIDIUS hardly efcaping by abfconding himfelf in a cave, was thence termed BRIDIUS, or GILEBRIDE of the Cave ; however after the king's departure he obtained new forces, by which he obliged the inhabitants of thefe parts to become his tributaries, in which he was not difturbed by king *Ederus,* then under fome apprehenfions of an invafion by Julius Cæfar.

BRIDIUS's fon was called SUMERLEDUS; for the chieftains of that clan were for fome ages defigned MAC SOIRLES, or *Sumerled's fons,* as Ri.Southwell, an Englifh writer, in his account of the petty kings, or Reguli, of fome of the Britifh ifles while under the dominion of the Norwegian kings, afferts, who fays, that thofe Reguli pofieffed all the ifles round Britain,

Britain, at leaft Scotland; thofe poffeffed by Sumerled's fon, being moft of the EBUDÆ, or weftern ifles then, and in after-ages pof-feffed by the Mac Donalds.

Anno 245 of the Chriftian epocha, in the reign of king *Findoch*, Donald the firft of thefe of that name found up-on record, made a defcent on the conti-nent of Argyle; but being defeated by the king, was killed with a great many of his men; for revenge of whofe death his fon of the fame name, in the year 262, and firft year of the reign of Donald the fecond, en-tered the continent with an army of iflan-ders. The king of the Ifles ufurped the go-vernment, and retained the fame for 12 years, at the end of which he was killed by *Crathilinth*, king *Findoch's* fon, who kept down his fucceffors, as did fome of the fucceeding kings; anno 762, one of the chiefs of the Ifles, called Donald, made an infurrection, but was defeated by king Eu-genius. The chiefs of that name poffeffed all that large tract of land, viz. Cantyre, Knapdale, and all along the weftern fea-

coaft

coaſt of Argyleſhire. Is it then probable, when the M'Donalds of the Iſles in Argyle-ſhire ſtruggled with one another, that the Scots Iriſh ſhould be ſuffered to land ?

And this faƈt will receive additional ſtrength from the conſideration that ABARIS, ARCH-DRUID of Liewes, was ſent an ambaſſa-dor from the iſles to Greece in the time of Pythagoras, about ſix centuries before the above æra, and converſed very learnedly at the different courts he was ſent to ; and from this cirumſtance it would be abſurd to deny that the iſles were either deſtitute of learning, or inhabitants.

And to make this good, let us remark what Diodorus Siculus obſerves : that, among the writers of antiquity, Hecateus, and ſome others relate, there is an iſland in the ocean, oppoſite to Gaul, not leſs than Si-cily, which is inhabited by a people called Hyperboreans, under the arƈtic regions, ſo called, becauſe they are more remote than the north wind. It is a fertile place, for they have a harveſt twice a year ; that they have a great foreſt, and a noble temple, where men, many of whom are harpers, ſing forth
the

the praifes of Apollo. That they had a language proper for themfelves, and had a great regard for the Greeks, which friendfhip had been confirmed from ancient times, particularly with the Athenians and Delians; and that fome of the Greeks came over to the Hyperboreans, and made them rich prefents infcribed with Greek letters; let Mr. P. liften with attention; and alfo that ABARIS formerly went from thence to Greece to renew their ancient friendfhip with the Delians *.

This defcription anfwers to no other ifland about G. Britain but Liewes, which equals Sicily in extent. Particularly, when it is known that the fea has fince encroached many miles on both fides (the country being flat) almoft within the memory of living people; eight miles are faid to be overflown; and black mofs is, at times, for political purpofes, dug up far below the fea-mark at ebb tide. No wonder if it was then as large as Sicily is at prefent, when it is about ·70 miles computed, 105 Englifh meafure in length, and in many places 18 or

* Diod. lib. ii. to the end.

27 miles

27 miles broad: and fome even imagine
that St. Kilda ifle was once joined to it,
though now a fheet of fixty miles of fhallow fea covers the intermediate fpace;
all which would make it equal, if not fuperior to Sicily in extent. The whole
plain is full of deep mofs; then it was full
of woods, with the grand arch Druidical
temple ftill to be feen at Callarnifh. And
that country, from the temperate climate, occafioned by the warmth of the furround-
ing feas, is fo extremely fertile, that the
Author has feen greens and other vegetables
fhooting out fix feet high at Chriftmas,
and after that time. And as to the prolific
nature of their cattle, whoever reads the
late Travels into the Hebrides, by Lanne
Buchanan, will be abundantly fatisfied of the
juftnefs of Diodorus's account on that head.

Plutarch alfo confirms their fending prefents and writs. That prefents were fent
with Sador, *i. e.* SAIDE FEAR, the archer,
that being part of the very drefs, afcribed by
another writer, as wore by ABARIS when
he entered Athens with his belted plaid
(a belt

(a belt gilt over with gold,) with a
bow and arrows in his hand. When SA-
DOR, from the Hyperboreans, went with
his prefents, he was accompanied with
beautboys, harps, guitars, pipes, and various
other inftruments. This is fufficient to
mark the country of that famous philofopher, who is alfo mentioned by many o-
ther writers *.

Mr. Aftle remarks, that the Phœnicians
came to the ifles for the article of commerce
more than 600 years before the Chriftian
æra; yet it does not appear, that they taught
the inhabitants the ufe of letters. Indeed,
fays he, the contrary hath been fhown by
Mr. Whitaker; and adds, that they carried
on their commerce with the Britons very
fecretly, infomuch that a Phœnician veffel,
when chafed by a Roman, chufed to run
upon a fhoal, and fuffer fhipwreck, rather
than difcover the coaft, tract, or path, by
which another nation might come to en-
joy their fhare in fo beneficial a commerce;

* Gaudentius Merula de Celtis Alpinorum.

and

and therefore it is prefumed that their policy prevented them from inftructing the
ancient inhabitants of Britain in the ufe of
letters. Neverthelefs, of this ignorance we
are told by Colonel Vallany, that the *Og-
bams*, or writings in cyphers, a kind of
fteganography, practifed by the Irifh, was
ufed, though it is not to be found in any
Dictionary of theirs at prefent ; but he very
judicioufly applys it to the elements of letters, and thinks it was practifed by the
Irifh Druids, even though he never faw
any Druidical writings.

This fenfible remark is much to the purpofe;
there is no reafon to doubt but that fuch a
learned body of clergymen would have committed their fentiments to writings, at leaft
many of them, tho' the misfortunes which
the revolutions of remote corroding ages
fhould befal thefe writings, as well as many
more of the fame kind, of much later date,
have been loft for ever to generations unborn,
long after this period under contemplation.

It is therefore a rafh conjecture in hiftorians, however dignified, without pofitive
proof,

proof, to aver, that the learned Druids committed nothing to writing, or that they were ignorant of letters, becaufe they have not furvived the ravages of time, and were handed down to our days fafely. They certainly had the knowledge of letters; and what we have feen above of the Greeks bringing them prefents, infcribed with Greek letters and writings, paffing between thefe people; and the learned Druids are fufficient to eftablifh thefe facts, tho' other corroborating proofs did not accompany them. Can any man of reflection hefitate for a moment to allow that fo learned a man as ABARIS, the Arch Druid of Liewes, who is allowed, about 600 years before Chrift, to have converfed with equal, if not more eloquence than any man in the Lycæum at Athens, and to have difplayed more knowledge under a belted plaid than Pythagoras under his cloak, could be entirely deftitute of the knowledge of letters, and of writing? To think otherwife, much more to write otherwife, would be an infult to people's underftanding. They then ftood in no need of

inftruction

inftruction to write from either the Phœnicians, or Greeks, as they were ofthemfelves
fufficiently qualified without their aid.

Befides it is certain, from the conqueft of
Alexander the Great, that Greek became
the univerfally received language almoft over
Afia, as well as Europe, and part of Africa;
infomuch, that the cuftom to write that language in Cæfar's time became very common
from the unequalled fmoothnefs of it's expreffions. The Gauls, he tells us, ufed
Greek letters, and he found in the rolls of
foldiers, their women and their children's
names were wrote in Greek characters ; fo
that for two or three centuries before Chrift,
it was the univerfal practice to write in
Greek, over all the weftern parts of the
world. We may fafely affirm, that in the
ifles of Britain commerce with the Greeks
made the language famous there, and the
intimate connection between the Gauls and
the Druids made them improve upon it ; and
it is certain that the Gauls traded with Britain from what Cæfar writes * ; becaufe he

* Lib. 4. de Bello Gallico.

O   conveened

conveened all the merchants, hoping for
foine fatisfaction in his enquiries about Britain, but in vain; thefe faid, they knew, or
pretended to know, nothing more than the
maritime coaft of Britain oppofite to Gaul,
their bufinefs being to exchange merchandife,
and to return, not to make curious remarks
on the extent of the ifland, the diverfity of
inhabitants, their difcipline of war, or the
commodioufnefs of their harbours.

All this, with more of their addrefs, is
truely offenfive in thefe Celtic cattle,
whether modern or ancient. The firft
have oppofed the *Fiks, Peukini,* or *Vic
Veriars* in the north, and this tyrant Bridan
and his fucceffors would not fuffer the Scots
from Ireland to take poffeffion in the fouth,
but drove out the very natives to make room
for his iflanders, and even his defcendants
extended their empire over all Scotland, afterwards, as is well known. How then can
Mr. P. give an account of the Scots and
Picts, when thus unexpectedly ftripped of
both ? No wonder he fhould rail againft
fuch favages, and more particularly againft
Bridan Mor, being the oldeft offender, in
occupying

occupying moft impudently the very place meant for the *Twa de Dunnan*, and the *Irifh Scots*, and for making him labour fo much in vain.

But they will have matters in their own way ; as Celtic underftandings will always continue to be Celtic underftandings in fpite of obftruction.

Dhanian co heridh e, in fpite of oppofition, an old motto of the Mac Donalds in their coart of arms from that time till now. This tyrant is juftly entitled to bear his own proportion of railing, feeing the Macpherfons have already got enough of that abufe.

Had Hæcateus, and other ancient writers, concealed the above account, matters would have fucceeded better ; nay, even M'Nicol muft open again like a Scheanachie, and fupport the old Gaelic too ; by telling the world that it has a regular and eftablifhed ftandard, as is well known to many gentleman of tafte and candour, who, tho' not natives of the highlands, have been at much pains to become acquainted with it. I fhall

only

only, fays he, appeal to two refpectable evidences, namely General Sir Adolphus
Oughton, and Sir James Fowlis; thefe
gentlemen will give a very different account
of the matter, and cannot be fufpected of
having any partiality; the one being an
Englifhman, the other a fouth country
Scotfman. The teftimony of Mr. Pennant,
and of every other elegant traveller through
the highlands, with that of the world, is in our
favour; and againft that, Mr. P.'s praife or
cenfure can have but little weight. What
Sir Richard Steel fays, with regard to himfelf,
may in fome meafure hold in this cafe, when
impertinent calumniators jealous of his fame
befpattered his character, as Mr. P. abufes
the Macpherfons and other learned men,
with the Celts in general; namely, that idle
people for want of other entertainment, and
difcourfes, muft be led to hate the perfons
of thofe they never faw, and oppofe defigns
into which they never examined. In one
word, one cannot but reprobate the ftubborn
malignity that this gentleman all along pur-
fues againft the learned and illiterate Celts,
and

and others, in his writings, when every
line is almoft marked with prejudice, and
every fentence teems with the moft illiberal
and unprovoked invectives. And I doubt not,
if he is thought worthy of notice: but he
will meet with fevere correction from fome
one or other of the abufed characters fo outrageoufly infulted by him. But the Author
would have taken his final leave, with the
fentiment of Agefilaus, refpecting the foolifh Menecrates, who ftiled himfelf Jupiter
in his letter to the king, with wifhing Mr.
P. health, and a found mind, did it not appear neceffary to make a few more remarks
before parting.

The acrimony of Mr. P. againft Macpherfon for mentioning the poems of Offian
and Fiangael, which he fo rudely terms a
falfehood, calls on the author to do juftice
to a fubject that has attracted the attention
of the indifferent, awakened the curious,
roufed the corruption of the critics, exercifed
the quills of the envious, and opened the
eyes and ears of the whole nation with the
ftrongeft defire and expectation of hearing

the

the genuine account of a fubject, that had gained univerfal applaufe, fully explained to their fatisfaction.

The fubject alluded to is the famous poem of Offian with the hiftory of Fiangael, and the Fians in general; and while the author reprobates the feverity of Mr. P. againft James Macpherfon, and hopes to be able to fupport the credit of the poem, yet he cannot approve of the laft gentleman's pertinacity, in filently refufing to Dr. Johnfon and others, a more explicit and fatisfactory account of thefe people and the poem, fo juftly allowed to have exifted manv ages prior to the publication of it by Mr. M: pherfon.

Dr. Johnfon, from his exalted character, as a writer, had a right to be anfwered refpectfully, the nation would then be fatisfied, and his own country highly honoured by a compliance to fo reafonable a demand.

But as it would be rude in the extreme to think he could not explain it fufficiently, fo, to fave him the trouble, and if poffible give fatisfaction to the reader, the author engages to unfold this feemingly myftical fubject, and

and leave with the judicious to determine how far the writer deferves credit from his knowledge of the ancient Gaelic language, and of courfe yield fatisfaction to the critics and others.

Here then before he enters on the fubject of the FIANS, or FINGALL, in order to explain it, it will be neceffary to premife that, in times of the feudal fyftem, every prince, lord, or laird in Scotland, was under the neceffity of protecting their private properties by force of arms; and each proprietor of eftates, whether large or fmall, behoved to keep a fharp look-out, as emperors and kings muft do at prefent, in order to protect their effects, by the incumbent vaffals and tenants, to prevent a furprife from fecret, no lefs than from the more powerful adverfaries, whether neighbours or otherwife; and thefe precautions were no lefs neceffary by night than by day, and the veftiges of thefe cautious fteps are well known to all fuch as underftand the language thoroughly, becaufe it is fo expreffive of the different objects and defigns, for which it

O 4   was

was originally intended. To illuftrate thefe by words and figns, and no lefs known now than then, though, to ftrangers to the idiom of that tongue, this affertion may appear ftrong and fingular, when compared with moft modern tongues that are changeable; but when it is confidered that this language never varies, the furprife will be leffened. It is true, the language may, and has given way to other tongues, for obvious reafons, as already obferved, in many parts of Scotland as well as in other countries, but ftill as much as remains of it, ftands unchangeably pure and is ftill the fame, and even a mixture with it is well known to be foreign, and quite different from the object expreffed, if mentioned properly in the Gaelic; in the mean time, the fact in affirming that this very ancient language is not a paradox, but a truth granted by eminent authors, will prefently appear.

The Scythian is faid to have laid the foundation of the Greek; and the Celts that of the Italian nation, as Leibnitz writes in Mifcellanea Bero, &c. page 5, &c. And to point

out

out the poſſibility of preſerving the language pure, like that of the ancient Chineſe, it is remarked that original languages have been beſt preſerved in iſlands and mountainous countries which are difficult of accefs, and whoſe ſituation is not ſo convenient for the frequent intruſions of barbarous tongues.

Of courſe the Britiſh iſles, ſays the writer, and mountainous countries have preſerved it with them, while other tongues, from time, are ſubdivided into a variety of branches *.

The ſame author proves from Ezekiel, that the Pelaſgi from the iſles of Eliſha ſold tin to the Phœnicians, which they had received from the Caſſeterides firſt, long before the Phœnicians were acquainted with the place ; nor is it likely they would pay profit to the Pelaſgians, if they knew how to come by it at firſt hand. And he thinks that afterwards the Phœnicians gave the name *Barratannac* to the iſle †.

* James Parſons on the antiquity of Taphet.
† Ibid.

From

From all which he feems to think that
the firft inhabitants of Britain came from
the Archipelago ifles *(i. e.* Elifha). This
gentleman remarks, on a paffage from Plato,
that the Greeks received their language
from the Pelafgians, among whom the
proper etymologies were to be fought for ;
and that if we go higher, we muft make
our laft appeal to the Creator ; and yet the
Greeks called the Pelafgi barbarous, becaufe of their tongue, which by fome is
fuppofed to have been Celtic.

He adds, that fome Hebrew words are
found among the Pelafgi, fo there was an
affinity between them, and declares that
there is little doubt, but the Phœnician
tongue had its origin from the Hebrew language. In Gaelic likewife there are Hebrew
words to be found ; as *Gael*, they called it
Gallim, and the Gaels term it *Gallin* *.

Having thus pointed out the poffibility of
preferving the Gaelic tongue pure and uncorrupted among the ifles and hills of North
Britain, the following explanation of the old

* Ibid.

FIANS

FIANS, and FIANGAEL will, I hope, gain credit, and yield fatisfaction.

The very name FIAN conveys the idea of a giant, or monftroufly ftrong perfonage to the minds of the vulgar, feeing they feldom mention thefe men, but in terms of awe and refpect, as if confcious from fome prefentiment, or unaccountable impreffions, that they were beings of a fuperior order which commanded fubmiffion and proper attention from their inferiors.

That this is the true definition of the vulgar and common fentiments of the Celts refpecting the FIANS, are facts fo generally received, that no one will controvert them.

This ferves as a key to open up what feemed a myftery before it was explained, and fufficiently points out how the plaineft language may be abufed by the ignorant, and may be rendered even unintelligible to knowing judges, by joining a combination of mifplaced words and fyllables ; circumftances which generally follow from the mouths and pens of men who are incompetent

tent judges of the true idiom and pronunciation of a language.

And no tongue has fuffered more than the CELTIC now under confideration, and that from the pens of writers who are otherwife able, but unfortunately remained ftrangers to the language of thefe defpifed and neglected people and their country; whofe hiftory they have attempted to tranfmit to pofterity for infallible certainty, though under this difadvantage themfelves; as might be made good, did not the fubject of the FIANS call off our attention to explain it.

Then this word FIAN is compounded of FIAU, *an alarm*, and AON, *one*; that is, an alarmed man, a man on his guard and defence. FIA NEACH are made up of FIAU, *an alarm*, and NEACH, *a people*; an alarmed people, or men on their guard or defence.

The AGNOMEN FIAU was an epithet given to them from their conftant profeffion of guarding and defending their country and property from the dangerous depredations of ftrangers, or from neighbouring kingdoms

and

and countries. In Englifh they were called *marchers* in after times; as the Douglaffes, the Kerrs, the Humes, the Cummins,
and the Maxwells, were fo named, while
they defended Scotland from the Englifh
plunderers; fo the Percies, Forrefters, and
others, who protected England from the
ravages of the Scots borderers were likewife
thus named. And the borders are ftill known
by the name of *marches*, or *merfe*.

The feuds that long fubfifted between the
kingdoms have been fo fully defcribed by
hiftorians, that a further account in this
place would be fuperfluous, as few common
readers have not been entertained fully with
the heroic achievements of the Douglaffes
and the Percies on the memorable occafions
in hiftory, and even fongs of the times.

After the fame manner the wild ridge of
rugged hills, which divided the Scots from
the Picts, is always called GARABH CHRIO-
CHAN, *rugged marches*; thefe were named
by the Romans, and are ftill called by
their followers *Grampiani Montes*, by
tranfpofing letters in order to make the
word

word found more agreeable to their Roman
ears; without regarding the real injury,
which fuch corruption offered to the abufed language, or that the very meaning
was materially affected by fuch improper
freedoms. Thus, inftead of GARABH
BHEANTIBH, they left an unknown
word in their ftead, which a highlander
cannot underftand, nor many fuch abomi-
nable tranfpofitions and additions to, or
cuttings off from the beginnings or ends, by
taking vowels out of, or adding vowels to
the middle of words, and interpolated expreffions as are in ufe, and explained by
their foreign figurative manner to their readers, by their *Prothefis*, *Apharefis*, *Syn-
copæ*, *Metathefis*, *Antithefis*, *&c.* all which
pompous figures and explanations have been
hurtful to every language, and more efpecially to the Gaelic, where every word is defcriptive and expreffive of the object it is
affixed to; and the above mode of alteration
has had the moft pernicious effect, as is well
known to every judge of the old Celtic.

Upon the whole, refpecting the Picts and
Scots, and before we put a final period to
this

this ftri&ure made upon the *Piéts* and *Scots,*
the kind reader will pardon the author for re-
marking once more with feeling regret, how
ridiculoufly the ableft writers may, and have
been led into the groffeft miftakes by relying
too unguardedly upon mifinformed authority,
while others with equal inattention entertain the world with conjectures of their own
fertile invention, and no lefs void of foundation, than of probability to build upon ;
this may be exemplified from the ftrange
account given of the inhabitants of North
Britain by fome fanciful writers ; fays one,
the firft inhabitants were Celts who poffeffed
that country for the fpace of a thoufand years,
or thereabouts, when behold a more favage
tribe called Cumri difpoffeffed thefe of the
whole country, except a few of the Celts
who fheltered themfelves in the mountains
and ifles of Scotland from the fwords of the
invaders, and where their remains are ftill
to be found.

The laft invaders enjoyed the poffeffions
of the poor Celts very fecurely, till, unfortunately for them a more ferocious tribe ftill,
(if

(if poffible) called Picts, poured in upon the Cumri about two or three hundred years before the Chriftian æra, who, in like manner, turned out the whole Cumri; and the few remains of thefe are ftill ex- ifting in the mountains of Wales. The Picts being thus left mafters of the field, were, however, in their turn deftroyed, root and branch, by KENNETH MAC ALPIN, and his Scots, who from the year 834 of the Chriftian epocha, continued in full pof- feffion of all Scotland, except what the Celts, (called favages by Mr. P.) keep poffeffion of in the ifles and mountains of the north-weft of Scotland. Now, can any dif- paffionate reader believe that any of the above, fuppofing them to have been diftinct people (a thing not granted,) would allow any new tribe to overcome them, after having had fo long time to increafe and multiply over the whole kingdom, and to be difpoffeffed of the country of their anceftors by fuch ftrangers; this would be granting a greater facrifice to thefe new tribes, than the PICTS, or CA- LEDONIANS did to the Romans, though allowed by all the world to be the moft

powerful

powerful and regularly trained troops on
earth, even with all their auxiliary forces
brought to their aid; yet we know that
thefe were obliged to retire, both with
fhame and lofs, after making the fierceft
trial; the very thought of reducing fuch
warlike people by any new invaders, is an
outrage againft common fenfe; and as thefe
could not, much lefs did Kenneth Mac Alpin
put a period to the Picts, as imaginary writers have inadvertently given out. We have
already, on purpofe, remarked, that the inhabitants were the fame; though ftrangers,
who have at different times heard new
names applied to them, imagined that the
inhabitants were equally new in the country,
as thefe prenomens were to their own ears.
Juft as Hollingfhed, fpeaking of the Scots
king's having invaded Northumberland,
about the year 1173, makes a difference
between the two nations under king William,
by calling him king of the Scots and Galloway men (or Picts), who, after paffing the
confines of the bifhoprick of Durham, did
much hurt and flaughter, with the additional

P   ruin

ruin of burning and fpoiling the country.
In the fame manner Everfden, fpeaking of,
the battle of Falkirk, anno domini 1298,
remarks, that the Scots, whom he calls archers, being flain by the Englifh horfemen,
yet though the faid horfemen affailed the
fpearmen, who ftood upon their defence,
they kept out the enemy by fighting man-
fully with their fpears held out like a thick
wood before them; they were at length
fore beaten with the arrows poured upon
them by the Englifh archers, infomuch
that they began to be in diforder, which
opened an avenue for the Englifh horfemen, and that gave the victory to the
Englifh; and finifhes that account by
telling that thefe fpearmen were men of
Galloway, or as the others meant, Picts,
by way of diftinction from the Scots, while
in reality they were the fame people, and
the different names were given for wife reafons, as above. We now refume the fubject of the Fians.

From the warlike fpirit of the Scots
highlanders, and their inclination to plunder
the PECHS on the eaft fide of thefe rough
marches,

marches, or the *Dorfum of Alabin*, neceffity required that certain princes, all along
the eaft fides of this ridge of hills, and even
on the weft fides of the GARABH BHE-
ANTIBH, behoved to be always on their
watch, both by nights and days, to alarm
the country, that the inhabitants might
inftantly repair to the ftandard of their leader, or FIAN, to prevent depredations,
and other fatal confequences, which generally marked the fteps of thefe bold agref-
fors wherever an attack was made.

And here it muft be remarked, that no
extraordinary reflection is meant againft the
Scots and Picts for thefe difagreeable advantages taken by either party ; becaufe that
feems to have been the common practice
followed throughout all Europe in thefe
early times, and that not by the commoners
only ; but alfo by their fuperiors in rank,
from whom better things ought to be exemplified. In proof of this we need only
caft our eye on the manners of the South
Britainers, where, according to Hollingfhed,
they at times funk into meaner practices
than either of the two former nations are

faid

said to have been guilty of. When speaking of the manners of the people, as late as
the thirteenth century, he says, these banditti, by confederating together, carried matters very great lengths, and all under the
mask of religion, supported by force, to ruin
the industrious inhabitants by their depredations; insomuch that the pope blamed king
Henry the Third of England for tolerating
of such abuse, and ordered to have the
guilty accursed, as too offensive to God and
man; for in the year 1232, matters went so far
forth, continues he, that there were sundry
persons armed and disguised like mummies,
which not only enterprised to take diverse of
these strangers who were beneficed men;
but also came to their barns, threshed out
their grain, and shewed counterfeited letters under the king's seal, which they had
procured for their warrant, as they did pre-
tend. At length the pope, upon complaint
made unto him of such violent doings,
wrote to king Henry, blaming him not a little for suffering such disorders to be committed

mitted within his realm; commanding him,
upon pain of excommunication, to caufe a
diligent enquiry to be made to find out the
offenders, and to caufe them to be punifhed
fharply, as an example to deter others : he
moreover wrote letters to the bifhop of
Winchefter, and to the Abbot of Saint Ed-
mondfbury, to make the like inquifition, and
to curfe all thofe that fhould be found cul-
pable within the fouth parts of England;
and the fame rigorous orders were put in
execution in the northern parts of the fame
kingdom.

Hereupon a general inquifition was
taken, as well by the king, as by the bifhops, and many were found guilty, fome
in faƈt, and others by confent; among
which number, there were both bifhops
and chaplains to the king, with archdeacons
and deans, knights, and many of the laity ;
there were fome fheriffs and bailiffs alfo,
who, by the king's commandment, were
arrefted and put in prifon ; and diverfe of
all forts did keep themfelves out of the way,
and could not as yet be found. In like

manner, Hubert Earl of Kent, Lord Chief Juftice, was accufed to be chief tranfgreffor in this matter ; as that he had given forth the king's letters-patent to thofe difguifed and mafked threfhers, who had taken on themfelves to fequefter other mens goods to which they had no right. There came alfo to the king one Sir Robert de Tuing, a knight of the northern parts, who had led about a company of the faid mafkers, protefting that he had done it upon juft caufe, to be revenged upon the Romans, who went about, by fentence of the pope, and manifeft fraud, to fpoil him of the parfonage of a certain church, and therefore faid he had rather ftand accurfed without juft caufe for a time, than to lofe his benefice without due judgment.

The plunderers of the South feem to have laid hold on fome feeming juft caufe of offences being received before they were provoked to commit fuch outrage on their fellow-fubjects, as indeed did the fierce inhabitants of the North, who never committed any depredations on their neighbours, without

without firſt announcing of ſome abuſe, or indignity, which they alledged as an ex-cuſe to colour their proceedings with a feeming ſhew of juſtice on their ſide ; the which behoved to be redreſſed at the ex-pence of their ſuppoſed enemies ; but as far as tradition, or written teſtimony goes, we never heard of the Scots or Piĉts making uſe of religion to cloke their knavery. At any event we may ſafely believe, if the inhabi-tants of Britain were ſo turbulent at ſo late a period, they muſt have been much more ſo many ages prior to the time under con-ſideration, and a proof that FIANS, or guardians were abſolutely neceſſary, par-ticularly near the mountainous countries of Scotland, where the inhabitants were more fierce than in the ſouth.

But to return to the FIANS, they had certain little eminences, named FAIRRE DUNS, (corruptly ſo called for DOWNS in Englifh) on which the centi-nel lighted a blaze by night, when any ap-pearance of danger approached, and the other inhabitants on feeing the fignal of dif-

treſs

trefs, immediately marched towards that place where, from the blaze or fmoke, they understood the danger was threatened. This was generally ufed as the moft expeditious mode of giving the alarm in places where the FAIRRE DUNS commanded extenfive profpects.

Where the country was more flat, or lefs expofed to the ftationary places of keeping guard, they ufed the fire-crofs, or *Croifh t'Arridh*, the flaughter-crofs; for ARRADH, in GAELIC, fignifies *flaughter*; and the dead left in the field of battle are faid to lie SAN ARRAICH, *i. e.* in the field among the dead. This name is well known, but corruptly in Englifh entitled *Slughorn*: with this fire-brand they ran from one to another with fuch velocity through the country, calling the people to arms with the word *Sluagh Ghairm* in their mouths (as above, *Slughorn*) namely, to call the people to arms; by this fpeedy proclamation the people were inftantly at the place of action, *Croifh Arridh*, as above; the firft was the figure of the fignal, the laft epithet means flaughter,

flaughter, a field of battle; HUIT N'-GA-
ISGEACH SAN ARRICH, *the hero fell
in the field of battle*.

This is the mode of giving fignals all over
the weftern ifles; every town and houfe in
an ifland know their own different places
for burning the blaze, or making a fmoke;
when any perfon wifhes to crofs from the
main land, or any other ifle, to vifit
an acquaintance, immediately the people
launch out their boats to bring over the
ftranger; and one of thefe fire fignals have
been feen in HARRIS, from Skye, a diftance of 24 miles; nay, there was a fignal
of diftrefs made on a certain melancholy occafion on the fummit of the high pike of
St. Kilda, and was really faid to have been
feen by fome of the inhabitants of the Long
Ifle, but they did not then underftand the
meaning, as the diftance of twenty leagues
was too long for fignals to receive a paffage
by them; nor could it have been feen, had
not the Long Ifle been flat, and in many places almoft on a level with the Atlantic. Our
furprife will be leffened at the method ufed
by

our predeceffors to colleft their forces, when
we find the fame method is ufed at this day
by a people nearly in the fame ftate and
degree of natural advanïage that our fore-
fathers were in, when the Princes and people were known by the appellation of FI-
ANS, and FIANEACH, or wardens and
guards of the kingdoms. And the ruins of
their great caftles are known to this time
by their names.

Tradition afcribes twelve, and a modern
writer fourteen towers to FIANGAEL;
and report fays, that he was buried at Kilin
in Brcad Albin, Perthfhire; in a word, that
appellative was common to many; juft as
the furname FERGU, properly fpeaking, was
to every king, or prince, as judge over the
differences among the people.

The reṃains of a large circular building
called the Black Caftle, are to be feen in
Mulin parifh at Erradour within a mile of
BALLY UKAN; near *Mulin* is another,
and many more towards Fortingale; but
the moft complete is that named CAIS-
TEAL N-DIU, at the foot of the hill

of

of GRIANAN, or GROUNICH CRUI-
NICH DUN, the gathering hill, or DUN,
being the place of rendezvous in the days of
yore; this veftige lies in the farm of CA-
ISHLY, weft from MINGINISH.

There are other caftles out of the line of
the other twelve, and connected with the
FIANS; one of them about five miles eaft
of KILIN parifh, above the high road;
the other called BORORA, about a mile
from ACHMORE, on the fouth of *Loch
Tay*, in the faid parifh *.

We fhall now take a wider range for a
little, in order to make it appear that this
order of men poffeffed all Scotland, and
that the name may, for any thing known
to the contrary, have then been as generally
received among the people, as the term
Scots is now applied to the defcendants of
thefe FIANS. In the fhire of *Sutherland*,
we meet with CAIRNNAM FIANN, being now a confufed mafs of immenfe large
ftones, the ruins of large buildings, which
lie in the parifh of *Dornoch*, about fix miles

---

* Camden, by Gouch.

to the weſt of that pariſh church. And in the pariſh of *Rougairt*, in the ſame ſhire, one meets with CLAISH NAM FIANN, about five miles north-weſt of the church. CLAISH being a narrow tract of country, and ſo named in other parts through Scotland, by way of diſtinction, from *ſtrath*, this laſt being of much larger extent. In this little diſtrict the guardians of the country were ſettled, with a chief in their neighbourhood called FIANN.

From the north of Scotland we paſs on to the ſouth ; and there, in Murray-ſhire, we meet with FIAN DORN, *i. e.* FINDORN, or the eaſt ſide of the GARABH CHRIOCHAN, or rough marches. And as this country lies open to the invaders from the north-weſt, it became neceſſary for the chief, who reſided here, to be well appointed with FIANNICH to attend him, when called upon to defend their properties from the enemy. *Findorn*, a well known town, is built on the ſea-coaſt, and a conſiderable traffick is carried on there, a much ſafer and more profitable profeſſion íion than the trade formerly carried on by the inhabitants in that part of the country, when the name was given to the place.

Near fifty miles north-weft of Aberdeen, in Bamfſhire, the caftle of FIANLETTIR ftands. This ancient feat of the *Fiannich* is well known from the honourable family to which it belongs.

This, with the country around it, was occupied by the FIANS, an armed company ready at a call when need required their affiftance.

We leave Invernefs, and haften to Perth-ſhire.

Then about two miles north-eaft from Blair in Athol, where that duke principally refides, we pafs a GLEAN FIAN DALE, the country where moft of the wardens refided ; and their chief moft probably lived at CAIRN DUBH, now reduced, like other caftles, to a confufed heap of ftones piled upon one another.

To the eaft of Blair Athol ftands caftle LUD, another of the old feats of the marchers of North Britain. The founder's name

name was LODDY, a man's name common then as well as in our own times,
viz. LEWIS, or *Lodovic*. Both the Lo-
thians derived their names from a prince of
this nation ; even London, by some fanciful writers, is said to have been so termed
from king LUDD ; and in Scotland there
is a *Beinn Loddy* in Perthshire, where many princes of that name are known to have
resided, about fifteen miles west of Sterling, in the bosom of a semicircular group
of high hills, and facing Edinburgh.

URR, ARD, a place situated on the
water of GEARY, about four miles east of
Blair, received this name from one of the
great personages who protected the country. URR, MHOR and URR, ARD,
were, and still are, applied to persons of
exalted rank and power over the highlands
of Scotland; and indeed this is the common way of speaking of them with strong
marks of respect : and very probably from
the *apex* of CRAIG URR ARD, the
watchman lighted his fire-signal to alarm
the whole party. to arm themselves against
the approaching enemy.

CAIRN

CAIRN DEARAG, and ESS DEA-
RAG, at Lannecaftle, where a great Fian once
lived, and the family is ftill upheld by their
defcendants, or relatives. Likely enough,-
Offian's DARGO, and other fortifications of
Fians or Princes may be met with, about
three miles from the houfe of Blair; and
about four miles fouth-eaft from the faid
Blair Athol, lies the famous FIAN CAS-
TLE, where a brave defender of that country once refided in thofe hoftile times.

Perhaps the reafon of fo many wardens
fettling here about Athol and its vicinity,
arofe from its being nearly oppofite to
LOCH ABBER, on the weft fide of thefe
marches, a place long known for the fiercenefs of its inhabitants, who frequently infefted the rich countries in Perthfhire a-
bout Dunkeld, and even the fertile Carfes
of Gowrie and Falkirk; that thus united
they might be able to ftop the progrefs of
thefe daring invaders, whofe fteps were
always marked with confequences dangerous to the natives, and efpecially to their
properties.

Fortingale,

Fortingale, rather FAIRE NAN GAEL, watching the highlanders: This place was once eminent for watchmen, and a ftrong body of FIANEACH were fettled a-round it.

At the head of LOCH TAY, in a nar-row valley, ftands FINLARIG, one of the Earl of Broad Albin's principal feats; a very ftrong caftle, well known to belong to the FJANS, and perhaps to FIAN GAEL himfelf, who is faid to be buried at Kilin, in its neighbourhood.

From the Grampian Hills to LOCH TAY in BROAD ALBIN, the river DO-CHART gently glides along through a beau-tiful highland ftrath of eighteen miles long, called by the name of the river; both fides of this valley are planted thick with gentle-mens feats, and large farm villages occupied by the inhabitants; in the happy neigh-bourhood of which we meet with STRATH FILLAN, rendered famous in more modern times, from the wells and waters of Saint FILLAN, which were believed to have been impregnated with the virtue of curing

lunatics,

lunatics, by that famous man; the place is on that account yearly frequented by people to reap the benefit entailed on thefe waters from the year 700 to the prefent; and the veftige of his old monaftery alfo remains, and is ufed for the fame valuable end with the waters, to contribute to the blefled purpcfe of conferring health on the diftrefled. But pafling this, we muft remark, that prior to this period the names of different feats ftill bear the name of the FIANS, as STRA FIAU LANN, where many chiefs under that defignation, accompanied with their vafials and tenantry kept ftrict watch againft the encroachments of the GLENUR-CHAY men, and thofe of the upper and lower LORN, on the weft fide of the rugged marches, and to whom the above STRA was always expofed, on account of its being an eafy open thoroughfare to pafs to the low countries of BALQUIDDER, STRATH of LANNE, and STIRLING.

In defence of which many fevere battles have been fought, as we are told from tradition, and even the fongs left for pofterity

Q   to

to recite, which might be marked in this place was it neceſſary to eſtabliſh the fore-going narrative from the ſtrength of ſuch authority ; but what already has been ſaid reſpecting the FIANGAELS will, it is hoped, ſatisfy any ſenſible reader of the truth of theſe wardens being employed in this kind of capacity, without additional ſtrength of il-luſtration to make the ſubject credible, or the name more generally believed to exiſt. And near the very Dorſum, or ridge of Alabin, in paſſing ſouth-weſt from STRA FILLAN, one enters into GLENFALLACH, or GLEN FIAU LAOCH, in Engliſh, the valley of the alarm-ed hero. Such a man is called a FAWARR, or a ſtrong man on guard.

This Fian defended the paſs that leads towards Lochlomond in the county of Len-nox. In the pariſh of Callander, Perth-ſhire, we meet with GLEAN FIAN GLA-ISH, or rather FIAN CHLAISH, a beautiful rich little valley, inhabited by the marchers, who protected the low countries of Mon-teith, and Strath of Lanne from the inroads

of

of the GLENORCHAY, or BALQUIDDER depredators.

In the adjoining Strath another chief lived at DRIP FIAN, in STRATH GERTNAY; hard by it. DRIP means active, stirring; and FIAN, vulgarly called *Drepan*, the name of a town.

LOCH FINN received its name from the same source; in the neighbourhood of which, one of the chieftans lived, perhaps at ARROCHAR ARR GHORADH, the slaughter hollow, to oppose the Argyleshire invaders, called EARRA GHAELICH, and in Cowal, further south, toward the end of the GARABH CHRIOCHAN, or rough marches, we find the castle of FIN NAB; NABI was, and is still is, the term for a neighbour through all the Ebudæ; perhaps it is more than probable that this gentleman had a few neighbouring assistants, to whom this familiar term was applied for their aid in time of need. FIAN CHRUACH, or the rock of FIAN, in the vicinity of GLENURCHAY in Argyleshire is well known; and we might follow the watchers in the same

Q 2 order

order over all the Weſt ſide of the GARAFII
BHEANS, as we did on the Eaſt, and could
eaſily mention ſeveral veſtiges belonging to
theſe chieftains, who were ſeated in their
regular order, to command the peace of the
kingdom, by forcing thoſe who were viola-
ting it into better manners by a ſharp appeal
to their broad ſwords, in caſe more mode-
rate and lenient meaſures could not inſure it.
But we ſhall rather paſs by to remark, that
not only the marches between kingdoms
required wardens, but even in the heart of
the kingdom, and over all the iſles, we find
that this order of men prevailed.

On the north of Campſay hills, the
country adjacent is called FIAN TIRR, or
Fintry, and the very pariſh is ſo named.
This place was infeſted by the inhabitants of
Clydeſdale and Campſay, and the whole
force of the country was neceſſary to protect
their property, eſpecially in ſheep and cows,
for which this country is famous. In Airſhire, not far from *Kilmarnoch*, another
country named FIANEACH, or *Finnich*, is
to be met with, ſouth-weſt from Glaſgow.

The

The Romans knew thefe inhabitants by the name of *Attacotti*, corruptedly fo called by them as ufual, inftead of *Aiteach Coitarin*, *i. e.* the cultivated country of the boatmen ; for *Coit* fignifies a boat, which thefe coaf-ters ufed generally for their fifhing and navigation ; the whole of the parifh is known by FIANEACH, a ftrong proof that danger threatened them by fea, and by land, and of courfe a ftrong band of defenders became neceffary on the weft coafts, facing the Irifh rovers and their curracks, in cafe they landed.

There is a Bo FINNAN in Dunbarton-fhire, where the village was planted by thefe guards. In Bothwell parifh, Lanercfhire, ftands CAER FIAN, corruptly *Carfin*; CAER fignifies a gentleman's place of refi-dence, it was fo ufed then, and is fo em-ployed at this day. Hard by Muthil is to be found a FIAN TULLICH, and another FI-AN TULLICH in *Glenlcadnag*, Comrie pa-rifh; FIN GLASSIE in Fife, and COR STOR FIAN of Niddry. FIN GASKIN, this laft quality added to FIAN reprefents the human mind with the idea of a brave hero,

Q 3   a very

a very needful accomplishment in a man
who bordered on a country, and even shire,
inhabited by FIANICH; all Fifeshire is
called FIAU, an alarmed country, as if the
natives of this rich country were continually
on their watch, to protect their private property from the surrounding plunderers, who
waited their opportunities to break in upon
this fertile garden of North Britain, to strip
the inhabitants of every thing valuable,
especially of their cattle. Fife anciently
was supposed to comprehend all the beautiful plains, from the Carse of Goure : on the
north of the Tay, to Falkirk on the south
of the Poull river, (ridiculously called Bodotria) by the admirers of the Romans.
So much in proof of the existence of a set of
gentlemen and vassals, who were denomina-
ted FIANS, as an agnomen given them by
way of distinction from their other names;
many of which prenomens, from the rust of
time, and the gradual influence, and corruption of ignorant and inaccurate speakers of
the language, appear now in the mouths of
people, clothed in a garb seemingly strange

and

and foreign, even to the moſt accurate judges in Gaelic.

But before this is exemplified, we muſt obſerve that the ſame government prevailed over the weſtern Hebrides, reſpecting the FIANS, and which is no inconſiderable proof that they were originally the ſame people. In Harris, Invernefs-ſhire, there is a FIANS BHA, commonly known in Engliſh by Finſbay; and between North and South Uiſt, Argyleſhire, ſtands conſpicuous pointing at both ſeas, the famous CRAIGNAM FIANICHIN, from the apex of which the protectors of that country made their remarks by looking to the ſea to prevent a ſurpriſe. *Loch nam Fian*, and *Coridh nam Fian* near *Dun Gainich, Benbecula, S. Uiſt. Cor na Fian*, *i. e.* the cauldron, or kettle of the wardens.

One inſtance or two more in the ſouth before we enlarge on the iſles and northweſt. On the ſouth-weſt of Lanne Caſtle we found Drepan, *i.e.* the active *Fian. Drep* or *Drip*, as above, ſignifying activity, or action, on the weſt in Strath Gertna, with

Q 4 an

another in the north hilly country, to give the alarm to the chief in cafe of danger; and at this Lanne, a third great hill for burying the Lannes, have been built, and called by that name LANNIBH-EUG, the *dead Lannes*. There is another DUN IRA, near Loch Eairn, called CUILLURNAN; *i. e. Cuil Jar Fiann*, the weft corner watch of Fingal, to prevent a furprife by the enemy, among the thick woods around the Chief's houfe at *Dun Ira*. From the whole it feems certain, as Mr. Knox remarks, that the whole country and iflands are filled with the exploits, and veftiges of Fingal's; fo that not only one but many men of this defcription of great heroifm and fplendid achievements actually exifted in the highlands at fome remote period of time. The numerous remarkable places that go under that name, is another ftrong corroborating proof; for we find the name and veftiges in Sutherland in the heights of the parifh of *Kildonnan*, or *Dun Fian*, as obferved by an intelligent clergyman from that country. There is a hill called KNOC FIAN, or

Fingal's

Fingal's Hill; and the people have a proverb, when there is a great falling off from any man in his fucceffors, whether in his family or office, they fay, Offian, the laft of the heroes. It is well known, fays Mr. Knox, that there are many poems and ftories in the highlands fimilar to that publifhed in the name of Offian.

In the ifland of Staffa, there is a fpacious cave of Fingal beautifully defcribed by Sir Jofeph Banks and Mr. Pennant. When we afked the name, fay they, our guide told us, it was called the cave of FIUN MAC CUILL, whom the tranflator of Offian's Poems has called FINGAL. How fortunate that in this cave we fhould meet with the remembrance of that Chief! as that ef the whole Poem is almoft doubted in England. At *Caol Ruidh,* in *Sky,* a found, one quarter of a mile broad only from Scotland, three miles from the mouth of *Loch Duich,* in Rofs-fhire, the ruins of a CAISTAL DUNNIN, that is, DUN FIAN, the hill of Fingal, are to be feen. There is

a *Dunnin*

a *Dunnin*, called *Torr Nawe*, near the heart of Strathern in Perthfhire, where another of the FINGALS lived, a beautiful large mound like a fhip, with its keel uppermoft; the Romans ignorantly called it *Terra Navis*, an earthen fhip: but in Gaelic, TORR NAOMBH, is a facred burial place belonging to the King or Prince who refided at DUN CRUB, the prefent feat of the Lord Rollo. There is fuch another large hill at Invernefs, where another of the heroes refided, called TOM NA HEURACH, the hill of the young men. EURAN ALUIN, is a handfome youth; here probably the young men were marfhalled by the King or chief FIAN. Near Lanny Caftle, be-weft Sterling, one meets with two places bearing the name; one at *Orbinn*, i. e. AIRRE BO FIAN, the watchtown of Fingal, in the braes above the chieftain's houfes.

Nay, another ftrong mark to corroborate what was hinted above, that the inhabitants were the fame with thofe over all Scotland; and on the north-eaft in particular, we faw that not only fingular bays

and

and towns are named by the epithet
FIANS, but whole diftricts in different
places evidently bear the names of the people there, though none of the vulgar natives can account for the inhabitants of
t' of tremendous ruins ftill fingularly at-
ti···

···y, we meet with BAILL NAIN, *i.e.*
BALLY-NAM FIANN, where a gentleman
refides. The many large BARPIANS in that
beautiful rich ifle ftrongly mark their exift-
ence in that country.

The BARPIANNS over all *Harris* and
Liewes are immenfe large Cairns of ftones
huddled and blended together into the
greateft maffes of confufion, and feem to
have been originally dwelling-houfes, and
poffeffed by the Fians; I fay, thefe are to
be met with in many places in thofe and
adjacent ifles, particularly at *Hellifhnifh*,
on the main land of Harris, and in the
ifland of *Scalpay*, and others, thefe huge
Cairns are numerous. Thofe above *Hellifhnifh* have been regularly built in the form
of a large fquare, comprehending fome

acres

acres of ground in the middle, perhaps
with a view to keep their cattle fecure in
the night from the neighbouring thieves.
Says Mafcow, among the ancient Scythians,
the flocks and herds, after grazing all day in
the open fields and paftures, retire, on the
approach of night, within the protection of
the camp, which confifted of wooden houfes
of the princes, which were carried about
in their emigrations on carriages by twenty
or thirty horfes and oxen, juft as the BAR-
PINS that ftood regularly fecured their flocks
in fquare fpots in the centre. And in the
ifle of Scalpay, or Glafs, fome of the BAR-
PIANS are to be feen to this day almoft in-
tire, ftanding quite erect in the middle of
other vaft confufions of ruined ones. And
one of the Englifh Gentlemen, a Mr. Haw-
kins Brown, who was fent to mark out
proper ftations for fifhing villages, did vifit
thefe old erections on the fpot, and can bear
witnefs to this affertion. This gentleman in
particular made the Author ftand within a
BARPIAN houfe, and he expreffed his utter
aftonifhment

aftonifhment at the uncommon fight of
ruins heaped together in fuch great maffes.

Thofe ruins have occafioned much fpecu-
lation among antiquarians, and the diverfity of opinions, is equalled only by the un-
certainty of individual conjectures on that
head. Various are the opinions, fays Dr.
Macpherfon, of the learned concerning the
intention of thefe Cairns, and concerning
the people, by which they were erected;
fome will have them trophies to perpetuate
the memory of heroes flain in battle, others
that they were erected in honour of Mer-
cury, the protector of travellers; others
fancy they were the feats of judicatures for
the old Britons; and others fancy they were
eminences on which kings ftood after they
were elected, fo as to exhibit themfelves to
the multitude. One or two critics think
they were boundaries which divided the
eftate of one great man from another; and
many have thought they were intended only
for burial places, to which laft opinion the
Dr. himfelf fubfcribes, becaufe fepulchral
urns were found in fome of them. This
indeed

indeed may be true respecting a few, but not applicable to such immense numbers of them as are to be met with contiguous to each other ; and as it were regularly formed like squares of built houses, fitted out for the residence of living inhabitants; differing in size, greater and smaller, according to the quality of the inhabitants; and even in Skye some of these rude buildings are several hundred feet in circumference, others have had but a smaller appearance, perhaps four or five large stones erected before the face of a hollow rock, like a small cottage in comparison to the more magnificent ones ; and they were certainly dwelling-houses ; neverthelefs, burnt bones and afhes might be found on floors, it being no ways uncommon at this day to burn the bones of fheep and cows, and fuffer them to remain there for half years and upwards, &c.

They were all built in circular forms, fomething like cones or fugar-loaves each, broad at the bafe, and gradually inclining towards a point ; and the fummit of each of which feems to have been covered with a large ftone to keep the ftructure firm. And

thofe

thofe large ftones are ftill to be feen reft-
ing on the top of each Barpian, as it
crumbles into ruins through old age.

Mounds of earth have been piled up a-
round thefe ftone buildings; and the one
kept pace with the other. Thus their heavy ftones were rolled up on the out-fide
mound, and gently placed on the wall from
thence, as it advanced in height, until the
whole was brought into a point, and covered, as already mentioned, by a bulky heavy ftone. In many places, thefe houfes
appear at prefent like great ruins funk down
within a hill in grofs confufed heaps; fo
that when the houfes were ftanding, the
inhabitants, in a manner, burrowed under
ground; and the green grafs, on the out-
fide of the mound, ferved for thatch to
keep the dwelling-houfes dry from rain-
drops in wet weather.

And it is not improbable, but the whole
inhabitants of Scotland and the Ifles, in
thefe warlike days of hunting, attending,
and herding of cattle, before hufbandry was
thought of, were called by the general name
of

of FIANNS; as, in after ages, they were called PEICHS, on the eaft fide, from their new imployment of farming the ground; and in the weft ifles, SCOTSH, from their *Sails*, or Scode, and fea-fairing bufinefs. That this was the cafe is pretty clear from many old adages in Gaelic, where the idea of war and hunting is ftrongly marked: *e. g. N-Roimh u San n-Feinn ?* Was you in the purfuit, or jeopardy to-day ?—*Bha me fan Feinn ?* I was in a meeting, or in an enterprize, &c. And a man's going to the FEINN is ftill underftood to be the fame, as his going on a very dangerous expedition. To this day that idea is ftrong among the vulgar, and exprefled in their old fongs, as is well known to almoft every highlander who fpeaks the language.

We now return to perform the promife of adducing one example out of numberlefs inftances that might be condefcended upon, where the Gaelic in the mouths of the ignorant has affumed an antiquated garb, nowife fuitable to the fpirit of that language.

guage. The inftance condefcended upon, for the fatisfaction of the reader, is
that of OSSIAN, which has occafioned no
fmall wrangling, and even raifed ill-hu-
mour, among the learned of late; and yet
this mighty word, when ftripped of its foreign drefs, will appear evident to the intelligent reader; and the myftery fhall then
appear nowife uncommon, or difficult to be
underftood.

Then, this name is compounded of
two words, OS or AISH, and JANN or
John. When one man addreffes his fpeech
to another, he always ufes the interjection
Os! as, OS JANN ! hearkye, John ! (it
is equivalent to the Latin word *heus,*
hearkye;) and fo to all other names of
men and women this interjection is ad-
joined. But in this particular word under confideration, AISH is applied, and
not OS, becaufe it implies a reflection of
things paft, or a prefentiment of futurity.
Thus, AISH-JANN means the reflections
of John; when John, or the bard, in compofing his poem, looks back on things that

R   paffed

paffed ages before his time, or anticipates circumftances that were to follow in after-times. Offian fays, in his TEMORA, After the mofs of time fhall grow on TEMORA, thou wilt endure, fays the bard of an-cient days, when reflecting back on old times. It is not certain, fays Mr. Smith, what bard Offian refers to; furely it was in remote ages even then. It is neverthelefs a proof that poetry, in the days of Offian, was by no means in its infancy.

And fome have imagined that great numbers of Gaelic tales were well known before this æra of verfe, and to fome of thefe Offian might allude with a melancholy kind of pleafure, when compofing his own poems by way of amufement in his old age; befides, the word *Shean 'aifh,* old way, or old fafhion, is the common mode of expreffion, when enquiring after one's health in any part of the highlands of Scotland; *Cinnas ata n'Dune ud n'diu?* How does that man do to day? the anfwer is, *San tean aifh,* in the old way, old ufe and want, &c.

And the two words, *Aifh Jann,* have
been

been time immemorial fo firmly united by
corruption, that even a judge of that language feldom thinks of parting them, fo
that they pafs under the idea of one fimple
root, though nothing is more inconfiftent
with the idiom of that tongue.

The inhabitants on the weft fide of *Dorfum Alabin* value themfelves on their being
Gaels, efteeming it a more honourable
name than *Gaill*, or *Goullibh*, the epithet
ufually given by them, to the inhabitants of
the eaft fide, arifing, as they imagine from
their fulky cheeks, which they fuppofe
them more eminently poffeffed of, than the
more pleafant Gaels, who are naturally
fprightly in their manner and appearance;
hence we are left to conjecture, whether
Fian Gael was, or was not, a native of the
weft fide of the *Garabh Bheantibh*, the common marches, and the anceftor of the Mac
Dougaels, this hero being named *Fian Mac
Dhuil*, by way of diftinction from others of
the *Fian Gaels*, fo frequent to be met with
in all other parts of Scotland; as *Fian Gael*
was the fon of Dougal, or *Mcc Dhuil*, the

grand

grandfather of Offian, the author of the incomparable poem, fo inimitably famous ; or
rather, if it was not for certain a common
appellative ufed both in the eaft and the weft,
as remarked above.

With regard to the authenticity of that
performance, fo much has been faid by
Dr. Blair, Mr. Smith, and others, in its favour, that it would be an infult on mens
judgment to litigate on that head, feeing the
internal, and external evidences are fo
ftrongly marked with fatisfactory truths of
its being genuine, that no competent judge
will ever attempt to reprobate it ; and
to anfwer the cavils of fceptics, ignorant of
that language and its merit, would be equally foolifh as fruitlefs.

Sir Adolphus Oughton, fays Mr. Bofwell,
our Deputy Commander in Chief, who was
not only an excellent officer, but one of the
moft univerfal fcholars I ever knew, had
learned the Erfe language, and expreffed
his belief in the authenticity of Offian's
poems ; but as Dr. Johnfon took the oppofite fide of that perplexed queftion againft
Mr.

Mr M'Queen in Sky, fo did he alfo at Edinburgh.

To prevent a difpute however, Sir A. O. who had a charming fweet temper, changed the difcourfe, as he found the Dr. would perhaps exceed the ordinary bounds of good manners before he would give up a favourite topic, in the fupport of which he had declared himfelf deeply interefted; and a rooted prejudice once entertained, can hardly be got out by the knowing and learned; this feems to have been the Doctor's cafe in an eminent degree, for he would rather allow the merit of that performance to fall to the fhare of Mr. Macpherfon, tho' averfe to that gentleman's fame, rather than that fuch a poem could be compofed in a country againft which he had declared himfelf openly.

The poems, fays Mr. Smith, which this gentleman, meaning Mr. Macpherfon, gathered from oral tradition, were certainly no other than thofe commonly repeated in the country, and in the manufcript he got from Mr. M'Donald in Croidart, out of the *Leabher Dearag*, or red book, together with

thofe

thofe he got from the *Bard, Mac Vurich*,
where the records of Clanronald's family had
been kept for ages back; the poems were
only more polifhed and better preferved in
the manufcripts than in the mouths of the
vulgar.

To this man's fentiments the author fubfcribes, having had frequent accefs of hearing
great pieces of them repeated, and was well
acquainted with John M'Leod, a native of
Harris, and a very aged man of 93 years and
upwards, who could entertain an houfe full
of hearers for ten days or a fortnight, with
thefe and other poems equally old, and fome
of them feemingly of more ancient date.

And for this piece of agreeable and inno-
fenfive entertainment, he was acceptable
company wherever he lodged, and generally
well attended with crouds of all ranks every
night, who liftened with pleafure to his
agreeable mufe. And that Mr. Macpherfon had merit in placing the different com-
ponent parts in the form he offered his tranflation to the public, is a truth fo generally
acknowledged,

acknowledged, that few impartial judges will venture to deny it.

The author however, never did hear the whole of thefe poems in the fame complete detail in Gaelic, except only in feperate rhapfodies, and each of which appeared to be a finifhed piece.

After thus difcovering who the FIANS were, and why the agnomen was applied to them by way of dignity, the reader, it is hoped, will hardly hefitate to allow, that each of thefe great perfonages would have their bards to ftimulate their men to the battle in time of trial, as well as to record regularly the mighty achievements of their princes's families, who employed them in his fervice. In regard, the want of thefe ufeful domeftics, would be placing the great chiefs who were the bulwark of their nation on an inferior level to their fucceffors, though under different names, as heads of tribes, or clans, yet their whole office was literally the fame with that of *Fians*, namely, to protect their people and country from the infults of depredators.

R 4   Speaking

Speaking of *Fingal*, Gibbon writes, that this hero's death perhaps, might anfwer to the 208th year of the Chriftian æra, when that hero is faid to have given battle to the fon of the king of the world, *Cargul*, agreeable to his fame, as handed down by the bard, and lately revived in an Englifh garb, when *Fingal* is faid to have commanded the Caledonians at that memorable battle where he obtained a fignal victory on the banks of the *Carron* near Falkirk, where the fon of the king of the world, *Cargul*, was defeated from his arms, after he had eluded the power of Severus along the fields of pride.

Something, fays Mr. Gibbon, like a doubtful mift ftill hangs over thofe highland traditions, nor can it be entirely difpelled by the moft ingenuous refearches of modern criticifm; but if we could with fafety indulge the pleafing fuppofition, that Fingall lived, and Offian fung, the ftriking contraft of the fituation, and manners of the contending nations might amufe a philofopher's mind.

The

The parallel would not be to the advantage of the more civilized people; if we compare the unrelenting revenge of Severus with the generous clemency of *Fingall*; the timid and brutal cruelty of *Caracalla* with the bravery, the tendernefs, the elegant genius of Offian; the mercenary chiefs who ferved under the Imperial ftandard, from motives of fear, or intereft, with the freeborn warriors who ftarted to arms at the voice of the king of *Morven*; if, in a word, we contemplated the untutored Caledonians, glowing with the warm virtues of nature, and the degenerated Romans, polluted with the mean vices of wealth and flavery; it is then fincerely wifhed and hoped that the account given of thefe heroes may, and will throw fome fatisfactory light on the fubject of the Fians, and difpel the mift which prevented that elegant hiftorian, as well as many others, from yielding a hearty affent to this feemingly myftical truth. What a pity but fuch learned gentlemen were well acquainted with the Gaelic, fo as to reprefent the fubject in a more mafterly manner before

the

the eye of the impartial public, than the author can pretend to.! In that case it is certain that Mr. Gibbon's doubts would not only be removed, but his masterly description would satisfy others that. *Fingal* lived, and *Offian* sung, and that the Scots then, as they still do at this day, deserved a better character both for humanity and the more tender feelings of compassion and good manners than the gentleman who gave rise to the preceeding animadversion on their manners, was pleased to give them.

The opinion of Mr. Hugo Arnot, in his History of Edinburgh, when speaking of Offian, and his poems, is more decided than that of Mr. Gibbon. To reject, says that author, the poems of Offian, we apprehend is impossible, so strong is the impression; yet to admit such dignified sentiments, such purity of manners, as have not prevailed generally among the most unpolished nations in the earliest and most illiterate stages of society, and which an observation of its progress has enabled us to form, is equally difficult to account for:

Had

Had this gentleman's refearches, however,
led him to enquire farther back into the real
hiftory of th. fe people in more remote ages,
he would have found out the fecret of their
being more learned and polifhed, long before
the æra in which Fingal live·· and Offian
fung; and alfo that the progrefs of civili-
zation of manners in thefe later ages was
on the decline then, from what appears in
the faint traces of it handed down by the
learned to our times ; fo that the age of Offian, refined as their manners then are allowed to have been, was not early, but
comparatively fpeaking modern. What a
pity that Mr. A. did not produce fome evidence to convince us of this ignorance of
theirs ; for fure enough the poems and other
fragments handed down by pofterity, difplay
both tafte and learning, even though they muft
have fuffered confiderably from the ignorance of thofe who handed them down from
his, to our times, and the writings compofed
by men of letters, have not furvived the de-
ftructive hand of time, from the more dark
remote ages for us to examine their merits;

rits ; yet this lofs is no proof of ignorance, much lefs of fuch marks of literature not having once exifted, (and the contrary has been made to appear from the teftimony of authors, though ftrangers to the Celtic language ;) but the real defign of Mr. Arnot in fpeaking of their ignorance appears in its full ftrength from the fevere attack made on the religion of the prefent times, by giving a preference to the Druidical over that of the Chriftian religion. When fpeaking of a people fo pure, fo honourable amidft their ignorance, he fays, that the dawn of arts, of learning, and of the Chriftian religion, fhould be accompanied with their degeneracy into grofs barbarifm is aftonifhing, and that Chriftianity with its introduction fhould confirm by example the truth of the doctrine it inculcates, namely, that a tafte for knowledge expels from a ftate of paradife.

We fhall not attempt to reconcile difficulties by fophiftical reafoning, but will rather reft under the mortifying acknowledgement, that altho' the fact undoubtedly fo ftands, we cannot fatisfactorily account

count for it. Here is a moſt unguarded, and, I had almoſt ſaid, unmannerly wound, deſignedly given to religion and its profeſſors, as if it had been calculated for the ignorant only, and that learning would diſqualify men from the enjoyments which are believed to follow as a reward ariſing from the laborious reſearches of the more learned, to crown their endeavours in ſearch of the truth with the happy fruits promiſed them for their pious endeavours. An outrage this, committed without even the appearance of probability or truth, and ſo groſs that it contradicts known experience, and a ſtrong proof that the heart of the man who could expreſs himſelf in ſuch terms, was ſtript of the vital feelings of religion himſelf, and wiſhed to impoſe his own lucubrations on the world as generally allowed ſtandards of truth, tho' nothing is more oppoſite to facts, as is too well known from the practice and converſation of the truly learned, who, through their ſuperior knowledge, are generally the moſt pious, the more learned they are : this was the caſe with a Newton, a Boyle, and a Milton;

Milton ; and fuch who are, and have been truly learned, are of courfe the nearer to a ftate of paradife ; while, on the contrary, fmatterers and pretenders to learning have all along endeavoured to laugh religion out of the world, and expofe to ridicule the fincere profeffors of the divine truths, while their own practice has rendered them objects of compaffion, and if their progrefs is not altered, they are marching on towards a different ftage from the fo much wifhed for paradife.

The manners, continues he, as reprefented by Offian are fo generally known that to defcribe them would be fuperfluous, nor indeed could juftice be done to them in an abridgement. To us is left the ungracious tafk to mark how widely fucceeding ages, in a more advanced ftage of fociety, deviated from the virtues of their anceftors, from what has been already remarked, refpecting the learning, with the politenefs and eloquence, faid to have been employed by Abaris, the Arch Druid, of the Ifles of the *Hyperborcales*, when at Athens and other polifhed

lifhed parts of Greece, as far back as the time of *Pythagoras*. Any of Mr. Arnold's readers may be fufficiently fatisfied, that learning in the more modern ages of Offian and other contemporary bards was by much on the decline, from what it was in former days; however much the refined manners of that prince may have excelled the more forbidding ferocity of fucceeding generations which continued to degenerate more and more, until they were funk into abfolute barbarifm and favage tyranny. Then, by degrees, the chains of the feudal fyftem were broke, and the ferocity of their difpofitions began to recover its primitive elegance of manners, which, in the days of Offian, are fo juftly celebrated.

Thus, for any thing known to the contrary, the progrefs of manners have repeatedly had, and may again as often have its infancy, its full growth, and its decline, as is well known to have been the cafe fince the times that Britain with its ifles have been firft planted with inhabitants. And it would be rafh to conclude that thefe early ages have had no

writings

writings among their learned, becaufe none of their monuments have furvived the ravages of time to convince pofterity how unjuftly their memories have been branded with unmerited obloquy and ignorance ; for certainly thofe who received, and could read letters written in Greek, fix centuries before the Chriftian æra, could alfo write and remit anfwers in the fame ftyle and language. And he muft be a novice in hiftory who has not read, that trade and commerce were carried on between the Phœnicians and inhabitants of the Britifh ifles long before even the Grecians heard or knew of that traffick to begin it themfelves; and it is believed that the old *Pelafgi* had been in poffeffion of that trade long before the ancient Phœnicians themfelves found out the fecret.

Upon the fhorteft reflection therefore the learned reader will at once admit, that the inhabitants of Britain, and of its ifles, could not tranfact bufinefs with thefe different people, without the neceffary accomplifhments ufually employed by others who have been bred to bufinefs, whether in the mercantile

cantile or military line of life. To upbraid
them with ignorance and want of letters in
thofe early times, and that in defiance to the
moft refined politenefs of manners, cannot
but affect the tender feelings of any confidering mind, and no fmall reflection on our
own modern grofs conceptions when we
pafs judgement too rafhly upon a people,
whofe qualities appear, upon trial, to be
equal, if not far fuperior to thofe of our
own. And when it is confidered how many
manufcripts have been loft fince the time of
Cæfar, which were then known to have
exifted, but now not to be recovered, yes,
even in Britain, befides other countries;
our admiration fhould ceafe from the moft
diftant thought or expectation of writings
that could not, from the nature of things, but
fall into ruin ages prior to the above period;
and yet from the agreeable remains of their
fweetnefs of manners, as we learn from
tradition and their fongs, which have reached
our times, if we judge of thefe as of others,
from analogy, we cannot refufe them when

S   poffeffed

poffeffed of fuch accomplifhments as have ftruck us with aftonifhment, to have alfo enjoyed the art of committing their words and actions to writing for the benefit of others.

But Mr. P. charges the Celts with an unpardonable offence, as they were and are ftill fo fond of Clans. What is praife-worthy in others, heaffirms to be almoft criminal in an highlander : whether in the right or wrong, thefe Celtic cattle muft be held always in the wrong.

That being the cafe, the author expects to be forgiven for illuftrating this tremendous piece of imaginary pride in them, and fo ftrenuouflly adhered to for ages paft.

Then this word *Clan* is the literal and common expreffion ufed for children, who on trial were, and will be found to have been nothing elfe but the offspring of the inhabitants of the eaft fide of Scotland, that being the place where the firft inhabitants on entering that ifland fettled their refidence. And when a prince found his eftate over-burdened with his vaffals and tenantry, he would,

would, as is moſt natural, turn his attention to ſettle a colony of them in the weſt
of Scotland, and afterwards as they increaſed
plant more of them in the oppoſite iſles,
being then vacant, and more immediately
under his own eye and protection, in caſe
they ſtood in need of his aid.

Moſt ſenſible writers were almóſt of
the opinion that the two people were relatives. Old Caxton, an Engliſh writer, of the
fourteenth century, when ſpeaking of the
Picts and Scots, in the times of the Romans,
ſays, that theſe people differed only in their
manners, the laſt being more deep and art-
ful than the former, but agreed in clothing,
and faith, and in courteſy of ſhedding blood ;
they covered their privy members with beer
rather than with clothing ; this exaggerated
account meets with the ſupport of Gildas
and Bede reſpecting the inhabitants of North
Britain, a circumſtance which plainly indi-
cates their affinity to each then. And if we
take a retroſpective view of their manners
further back through the dark ages of antiquity, the greater will their conformity

S 2   with

with each other appear, till by tracing one generation after another in thefe more remote times, the higheft and firft emigrations among the different tribes, would be literally found to have ftepped forth from the firft fettlers on the eaft fide of North Britain, as juft now remarked.

The Caledonians would, as is moft natural, fettle their firft colonies in their own neighbourhood, and enlarge their boundaries to the weft in proportion to their ftrength and increafe; and by gradual progreffion remove farther from their fathers to fupply the uncultivated weft coafts and numerous ifles with new inhabitants; and notwithftanding the diftant ages, the language and drefs of both nations continue much the fame, as Caxton writes of them in times of the Romans.

Thither he fent his own fon called *Mac*, and the children of his vaffals and tenants, called *Clann*, to fettle in thefe uninhabited places, accompanied with a ftock of cattle, in proportion to their different ranks; and by following the example fet before them

by

by their parents, they would foon be
in a condition to make a livelioohd, and
multiply fo faft as to be able to defend themfelves with little more affiftance from their
patents. That this was the mode followed in thofe early times is not only probable, but it is almoft certain, from a fimilar practice ftill in ufe in the weftern Hebrides, among the vaffals and tenantry who
inhabit thefe ifles.

As an additional proof of this, I will firft
obferve, that gentlemen and rich leafeholders, who are fettled in the beft parts on
the coaft fide, generally plant the coaft fide
oppofite to their own farms with favourites,
or tenants, and every fuch farm comprehends
the whole intermediate tract of country, whether hills or plains; and the narroweft of thefe
ifles is about five computed, or feven and a
half miles of Englifh meafure long, and many
of them much more extenfive, as may be
known from the maps and geography of
the Long Ifland. Thefe cottagers, or lefs-
er tenantry, are planted at prefent along
the extenfive coaft of the royal foreft in

S 3   Harris

Harris, and called the back fettlements of thefe wilds.

And this mode of planting uninhabited diftricts was not only the moft rational practice firft ufed in Scotland, but it is almoft clear to a demonftration, that a prince, who was poffeffed of a certain tract of lands on the eaft of *Alabin*, was in like manner proprietor of the hills and forefts adjoining, even to the oppofite fhores on the weft fide, and alfo of the contiguous ifles in proportion, as thefe alfo lay more convenient to his eftate, than they did to that of any other fettled at a greater diftance; and doubtlefs when any one encroached on the remote parts of another man's property, war was the confequence; and the appeal for the real right was at laft made to the longeft fword, which ultimately put an end to their differences and feuds.

To thefe, as remarked above, the fon of the chieftain, with the children or Clans of the vaffals and lower tenantry was fent; and thefe were naturally fupported by their parents from the eaft with all their ftrength,

in

in cafe ftrangers began to infult them from remote quarters. This mode of planting the highlands and ifles, is not only the moft likely, but the ufual manner practifed at this day in thofe places which are as yet next to a ftate of nature. We may in a manner infer that the ancient cuftom of the original inhabitants is made the rule of their actions in many other particulars.

Nor is it probable, that ftrangers would be permitted to force themfelves on thefe young colonies then, more than at prefent. Then when we read of *Dalriads*, *Tua de Dannans*, names without meaning, and Irifh Scotch, fixing their refidence in the fouth of Argylefhire, the moft fertile fpot of the weft highlands, we may juftly call in queftion the authenticity of the hiftory of thefe imaginary fettlers ; more efpecially about the year 503 of the Chiftian æra, when the pofterity of the iflanders and high-landers had fo effectually feated themfelves, and were become fo numerous that room was wanting for their comfortable living to-gether over all the weft of Scotland ; info-

much

much that they had almoft proved too many for the very Picts on the eaft, and had exerted their ftrength to drive out thefe inhabitants, to plant fome of their own numbers in their ftead, as is too well known from the trial made, when Fergus the Second, with the Scotch, was expelled the whole kingdom.

Now it is impoffible that the Irifh Scots are here meant to give battle to the Picts, becaufe, according to Mr. Baxter's account of thefe, their numbers were fo few as hardly to be known, and as Ravenant the monk relates of them, they were fo obfcure as not to be known till after the feventh century.

Adeo obfcuri nominis ut jam feptimo, exeunte fecula vel ignoti fuerant, aut neglecti. On the contrary, Ireland was peopled from Scotland, and this in a great meafure appears from their patronimicks. As the iflanders and highlanders are called *Macs* and *Clanns*, fo the Irifh chiefs are commonly named *Os*, or grand-children, as if the fecond colonies fent by the inhabitants of the eaft and weft of Scotland were fent thither to make fettlements there, as the Macs were at firft fent

to

to the ifles. Thus we meet with *O'Don-nels*, *O'Neals*, *O'Harras*, *O'Keans*, and numberlefs others named after the founders of thefe names. On the fubject of *Os*, or grandfons, we do not intend to infift more at prefent, nor defire any one to embrace a conjecture, however plaufible, without au-thority to enforce it, only we leave the fen-fible reader to judge for himfelf. This is cer-tain, however, that the Earl of Antrim's progenitors went over from the weft of Scot-land at a much later period, and retained the name of *Mac Donnel*, which is ftill kept up in the family to this day.

Be that as it will, we may appeal to the fenfible reader, whether thefe tender and endearing terms of *Macs* and *Clans*, ufed among the highlanders, are taken in a natu-ral, religious, or political fenfe; I fay, let the tender feelings of every unprejudiced perfon be confulted, and anfwer whether their fpeech is not highly prudent and praife-worthy, fuppofing that their chief addreffes thefe lower orders as his deareft children,

like

like parents, or as kings, who are fathers of their people, and nurfing fathers to the church in a religious point of view. Can Mr. P. himfelf devife a more endearing tye by which a prince could fix the whole of his fubjects firm in his intereft in the day of trial and battle? Could any mode be fallen upon more effectual to eftablifh his throne in the hearts of his people? Let Mr. P. anfwer or confute this truth if he can, or with a blufh confefs that his violence had led him into an error in fpeaking fo unguardedly of a wife and brave people.

There is a vicious fingular animal of this defcription, who has made a kind of livelihood for years, partly by impofition, and moftly by entertaining the publick with malignant effufions of his own invention, at the expence of characters of worth and learning, efpecially if they are unfortunately of this intermeddling bufy body's acquaintance, and among others Mr. P. himfelf is faid to have alfo felt his fatire. People are not certain whether this Proteus may not be the fuppofed author of a book entitled Dr. Anti-pudingaria,

pudingaria, and to be feen in the Britifh
Mufeum; but Dr. Antipudingaria is lefs
manly than Mr. P. inafmuch as he dares not
attack a man under his own proper name,
but like the monfter, who lately infefted the
ftreets of London, by ftabbing defencelefs
women as they paffed along, and fecretly
rejoiced in this fuccesful mode of affaffina-
tion; fo, in like manner, this Dr. Antipudingaria fecurely affaffinates the reputations and
tarnifhes the learning too of his acquaintances,
efpecially if men of merit. In his ufual crafty
manner he addreffes the publick in the third
perfon fingular, or in the plural number.

This mode he is known to follow by way
of take in, that the reader may think the
general voice fpeaks the fame language,
which he thus fulfomely belches forth thro'
his own malignant throat, into fome magazine or newfpaper; however, the effects of
his poifon are not now fo deadly as he could
wifh, feeing that his real fpleen and defign
are pretty generally known among the difcerning readers ; and the moment a fatirical
reflection is uttered abroad, many of the readers,

ders at leaſt enquire whether Dr. Antipudingaria has any hand in ſuch and ſuch publications ; if anſwered in the affirmative, then
leſs credit is yielded to the paragraph in the
paper thus degraded by him, and announced
to the public as faɛts ; and of courſe he has
loſt his aim (of *Calumniare audacter, aliquod
adhærebit.*) And for this infamous praɛtice
ſome of his employers have diſcharged him
from their ſervice, for diſgracing their papers, hurting their private intereſt, and
wounding their own charaɛters in the eye of
their cuſtomers ; but he is no ſooner drove
out of one place than he hops into another,
until drove out from thence. People are
of opinion that he has fortified himſelf lately
about the Engliſh Review, ariſing from
ſome dirty eruɛtations that have been belched
out in that publication, very like the malevolent ſpirit of Dr. Antipudingaria,

It is ſaid that one out of this claſs of men
attempts to aɛt the part even of a critic and
reviewer ; but ſeeing that office requires extenſive reading and laborious reſearches) a
trouble noways agreeable to a man who has
little

little time and lefs inclination to fpend on
that fatiguing exercife); he ufually is known
to take the more eafy mode, either of be-
fpattering, or flattering characters injudi-
ciuofly, juft as he is, or is not friendly difpofed
towards the author. By way of criticifm on
a learned work, we therefore read, of a Mac
Gregor, hen-pecked, gluttony, a guardian
of money, miffionary, and fuch like, to fupply the want of abilities for the time. As
the author finds it difficult to prevail on an
editor to infert an anfwer in the fame vehicle
where he himfelf has been infulted by this
lame member of the fraternity that falfely befpattered his moral character, inftead of cri-
ticifing on his work, as this critic ftands much
in need of protection from the fevere lafh of
a juftly offended fufferer.

He muft then once more claim the reader's
indulgence to explain the meaning of the
word Miffionary-Minifter by way of defence
againft this eminent critic.

In order to this he remarks that there are
two kinds of temporary offices in the church
of Scotland, and the candidates are equally finifhed

nifhed in their education with the moft learned in Britain; thofe fituations are fupplied by
young preachers before they receive a fettle-
ment in that church; and rather than be un-
employed, a young man thinks himfelf fortunate if either his own abilities, or the intereft
of friends can fecure him one of the two. That
of a miffionary is by far the moft eligible, becaufe the preacher is fupported by the royal
bounty, and has a feparate diftrict or parifh,
and congregation of his own, and is, on that
account independent, and equally refpected
with any fettled clergymen in the church.
The author was in poffeffion of the very
firft and beft of thefe in his majefty's gift,
and hopes that his appearance in publick will
convince the fenfible reader that his literary
accomplifhments are little inferior to his
enemy at leaft, and fully anfwerable to the
high honour conferred upon him by that
learned body in appointing him to fuch a
charge.

The other, but much lower and more difagreeable office, is that of an affiftant or
helper to fome aged or deranged minifter; the
helper's

helper's falary is lefs, and more precarious commonly ; becaufe he is at the mercy of a poor minifter who cannot afford much pay out of a yearly ftipend of 60 or 70l. and may be turned off at pleafure by his mafter, who is generally fo jealous that the fituation of the poor helper is often embittered, and fometimes infupportable. This clafs of men are much worfe off than the loweft order of the Englifh curates, and being thus under the mercy of others, they often leave their birth and go in queft of better bread to London, or elfewhere, as Providence may order their lot.

When one reads in the Englifh Review of a miffionary, and reprefented in fuch fpiteful contemptible terms, a reader would naturally look on the office as infignificant, and that a very learned but offended dignitary only could venture to exprefs himfelf againft an enemy in fuch faftidious terms as L. B. is handled in that abufed vehicle. No man would believe that one who has efcaped out of the low order of helpers, would take leave of his fenfes fo far as to prefume to

ex-

exprefs himfelf fo unguardedly impudent; yet what fhall the reader think, when, with a blufh for the extreme corruption and depravity of the human heart, it muft be confeffed, that the real author of this outrage, when his name is given up, happens to be one who has fled from the above low rank, and who under a cover entertains the publick at the expence of his benefactor and fuperior; *Rifum teneatis amici!* And any curious reader who doubts the above fact has only to enquire of the Rev. Dr. William Thomfon, Fitzroy Street, and he will, from his own fad experience, fully fatisfy him, feeing the Dr. himfelf during the time of his minifterial office could never mount higher than the ftation of an affiftant to an aged poor clergyman.

Upon the whole, we may fafely draw this inference from the above ftricture, namely, that the abilities of a learned critic are known by the general rule he lays down to himfelf in judging of the work, rather than the character of an author; this is one infallible mark of his extenfive reading, efpecially if

it

it is equal or nearly fo to that of the author, then his judgment is impartially given to the publick, for or againft it, as the work deferves.

On the contrary, fmatterers, who are a difgrace to that learned profeffion, as if confcious of their own want of abilities, give up the work, and immediately dabble at the author's character, regardlefs of truth or falfehood. And this is all that can reafonably be expected from their limited capacities, to fill up their papers. A very pretty penny-worth to the purchafers, fure enough, to be entertained with for their money ! Meantime the author has reafon to thank the learned critics, who fpoke refpectfully of his Travels, all of them except one feeble pretender to that office, whofe intemperate rage proceeded from a well known, tho' unexpected difappointment, in order to prejudice the reader againft his future performance ; and all this owing to the fortunate refult of an early and friendly precaution, by which the author has been preferved from

T   difagreeable

difagreeable confequences ; and he means in future to benefit from the kind admonition.

A fine fpeaker, and no lefs elegant writer, remarks, in a fet oration on fuch beings thus ; namely, that the moft dangerous, as well as the moft infamous of all animals, is the flandering defamator of characters; within the fphere of his attraction no perfon is fafe ; the objects of his attact are either his enemies, friends, or perfons indifferent to him. The firft of thefe, from cowardlinefs, the natural offspring of cruelty, he dares feldom engage ; the fecond, if a plain and good-natured perfon, he roafts and tears with fecret joy, void of remorfe, inftead of prudently protecting his benefactor ; if quick and and animated, back-biting either by word or writ, is his fafeft mode ; as for the third, who never did him harm in thought, word, or deed, him he ftabs with an indifferent hand, like his brother monfter who lately infefted the ftreets, and ftruck terror over the whole city, until he was detected in the mean mercilefs practice of ftabbing defencelefs women, and immediately

ately fecured. This Timon, fays he, like a fecond Cacus, fhould be dragged into light and
expelled from the fociety of men, and drove
to the deep receffes of the woods, and forefts, to take up his abode in dens and ca-
verns, the ufual haunts of other wild beafts,
as tygers, wolves, and bears, to roar, grin,
and growl, and tear, and deftroy one another.

For the prefent, however, we fhall leave
this oddity, to put in a good word for one
more of the many learned gentlemen who
have been roughly handled by the more bold
and manly, though lefs dangerous, Mr. P.
who dares face a dead as well as a living adverfary with courage, *in propria perfona.*

' Buchanan,' fays he, ' quoting a paffage
' from Eumineus's Panegyrick upon the vic-
' tory of Conftantius over Alleƈtus, an. 296.
' viz. *adhuc natio etiam tunc rudis et foli Bri-*
' *tanni*, underftood that word in the genitive
' cafe; ftrange, continues he, fo able a latinift
' fhould fuppofe *Britanni* here ufed adjec-
' tively, while *Britannicus*, and not *Britan-*
' *nus*, is the only word ufed in profe in that
' way (*i. e.* adjeƈtively).' Well, indeed, may

the

the Macpherſons and others bear with the
the abuſe thrown out againſt them in common with many of the ableſt Scotch and
Welch writers, who are ſaid to ſee with
the jaundiced eyes of ſickly antiquiſts, when
they hear of the fabuliſts, Buchanan and
Llhuyd, the firſt the ableſt latiniſt and poet,
the other the ableſt antiquarian, ſo roundly
uſed.   Iſhmael has drawn his ſword againſt
every man ; what ! not ſpare even the elegant Buchanan, as Dr. Johnſon calls him ?
Buchanan, the pride of his name, the honour
of his country, the ornament of great Britain,
and the admiration of all Europe, who con-
feſſedly had neither ſuperiors nor equals ſince
the Auguſtan age ; yet he muſt be alſo called in queſtion for his ignorance in claſſical
knowledge, a quarter in which he is allowed by all to be invulnerable, and by a
man too whoſe knowledge in proſe and verſi-
fication appears to be limited and inaccurate.

One would imagine that Buchanan's barely adopting the word would of itſelf ſtamp
it with authority, even if he had not been
ſupported by Cæſar and Tacitus, and all the
learned

ancients or moderns. How would thefe injured men growl had they been alive, and
fwallow him and his works at one bite,
without falt or fugar, to qualify the bitter
morfel, and hurl both into oblivion.

Britannus, if applied, as a chriftian name
commonly is, to a perfon, will be admitted as a fubftantive, but when ufed otherwife to men in general, or to other fubjects,
as in the paffage already in difpute, I maintain, againft Mr. P. that it cannot ftand in a
fentence without a fubftantive; and add,
that *Britannus vir* is more elegant than *vir
Britannicus.* To oppofe fo high an authority as B. is a bold undertaking indeed !

Before Mr. P. few men in their fenfes
ventured to find fault with Buchanan refpecting his claffical knowledge, except the
foolifhly vain Dr. Liefiemmi, a phyfician,
who accufed that great poet with bad Latin
and poetry, and made no fcruple to prefer
his own tranflation of the 104th Pfalm to
that of Buchanan's, and appealed to the Univerfity concerning the juftnefs of his criticifm on B.'s, as mentioned by Mr. Granger,

T 3   under

under the title of *Poeticum Duellum;* juſt as Mr. P. has done to the public reſpecting *ſoli Britanni,* as being always a ſubſtantive in proſe, a remark which no body has thought worthy of notice to correct him for, being ſo egregiouſly wrong, and of courſe below reproof.

The Dr. however was better heard, as being no deſpicable Latin ſcholar, ſo B. himſelf paid attention to his criticiſm; and accordingly entered,the liſt againſt him,in a little performance under the above title of *Poeticum Duellum, ceu Georgi Egliefimmi cum Georgio Buchanano pro dignitate paraphraſeos,* Pſ. 104. *certamen: cui adnititur Gul. Barclay amœniorum, artium, et Medicinæ Doctoris, de eodem certamine judicium, necnon conſilium collegii medici, Pariſianis de ejuſdem Egliſiemmi mania. Quod carmine exhibuit Arcturus Johnſtonus.*

In this literary duel the feeble Dr.'s pride was dreadfully mortified with great humour on B's ſide, who at the ſame time left his opponent's character wounded with ſuch ſcars as ſtill remain incurable ; eſpecially as the deciſion of the judges on this curious

trial

trial was paſſed ſo decidedly againſt him, namely, that it would be more difficult to find in Buchanan's tranſlation any verſes that are not good, than to find any in Egli-eſimmi that are not bad.

Dr. Robb ſays, that the elegance of B.'s ſtyle was ſuch as would place him on an equality with the moſt admired of the ancient writers; and Dr. Burnet declares, that he not only far exceeded Bembo, who attempted to reſtore the purity of the ancients in his writings, but that one would be tempted to prefer Buchanan's tranſlation even to the original in point of elegance and purity of compoſition. Dr. Abercrombie writes, that Buchanan was an incomparable ſcholar, and eminent maſter of the Belles Lettres and Latin tongue, a celebrated poet, and a judicious hiſtorian.

Sir Robert Sibbald, writing of B. ſays, *Alterum Scotiæ lumen fecit Georgius Buchananus, poeta incomparabilis, qui oda, elegia, tragedia, non ſolum ſeculi homines ſuperavit, ſed antiquiſſimus equavit;* viz. that B. was not only an incomparable poet, who excel-

T 4   led

led in odes, elegies, and tragedies, all the men of the age, but that he even equalled the moft ancient, being the other luminary of Scotland.

After fuch remarks, it would be fuperfluous in me to attempt a defençe of B. from the attack of·Mr. P. as he is far beyond my praife, and above fuffering from his trifling cenfure; but my real defign is, if poffible, to correct Mr. P.'s vanity, and point out his feeming ignorance of that language, and his injurious reflections, together with his inaccurate curfory manner of reading fo many thoufand volumes as he tells the world he has done, on purpofe to upbraid Dr. Macpherfon for his limited reading, as having no library to lay up a ftock of knowledge to bring out materials occafionally as need required. For undoubtedly his inaccurate reading will appear evident from his paffing over the following well attefted particulars, before he would venture his own reputation in challenging fo great a character as Buchanan;

otherwife

otherwife he could not have the effron-
tery to deny, that *Britannus* is as much an
adjective as *Germanus, Romanus, Battavus,*
with all general names of nations, that are
always taken as fuch, and never once as a
fubftantive, except when fuch adjectives
fupply the places of fubjunctives (with fub-
ftantives underftood) which agree with them
in gender, number, and cafe: e. g. *patria,*
one's native country *(fupple terra)*; *molaris,*
a milftone *(fupple lapis)*; *triftes,* a fad thing,
(fupple negotium) *. Camden fays, that *Britannus, Britannia,* and *Britannicus* fignify the
fame thing; but as this felf-fufficient man
has fo decidedly told the contrary to the
publick, he will not believe words without
producing pofitive proofs againft his opinion,
and fuch as will force conviction on his mind
to make him confefs (at leaft tacitly)
that either ignorance, or which is worfe, ob-
ftinacy, hath caufed him to expofe himfelf,
and fo unguardedly to miflead his ignorant
readers.

* Vid. Rud. Reg. 15 Etymol.

W.

We fhall then begin with Cæfar, and try whether he underftood *Britannus* to be an adjective or fubftantive: *Omnibus ad Britannum bellum rebus comparatis*, Cæf. Comment. lib. 5. *Britanni vectigalis*, ibid. *Ut Britanni ad fpem, ita veterani ad metum trahebant*. As the laft of thefe is an adjective, fo muft the firft be of courfe, being coupled by the conjunction *ita* ; therefore, *milites* is underftood to both, and the nominative cafe to the verb, *Tacitus Annalium*, lib. 4. cap. 32. *Galfridus monumetenfis de origine et geftis Regum Britannorum*, Par. 1508. Britifh Mufeum. *Britannos relinquere liberos magna cum ignominia cogantur*, Boet. lib. 4. *Romani ignari Britannos Reges multarum in populo feditionum et rebellionum in fe fuiffe authores*, ibid. lib. 5. *Nam quid Britannum cœlum differe putamus*, how different is the air of the Britifh ifle, *Lucretius*. *Cui pelle falum fulcare Britannum*, who oft in leathern boat on Britifh fea appeared, *Sidonius Appollinaris*. *Proculque fe oftenderit claffe Britannia per Rhenum Oftium*, Grotius Antiq. Bataviæ, cap. 17. page 264. *Romani tamen dum fugientes*

gientes per stagna lacus; *saltusque Britannos avidius insectantur*, Elenchus Antiq. Albion per Danielum Langhornium, *page* 88. Erat ille vir nobilis veteri Britannorum Regum prognatus sanguine, *ibid.* 177. A gadibus usque Britannum reversus oceanum terruit, *Pampinianus status ab Arngrimo Jona Islandia*, p. 101. pars 2. Indeque ad socerum Britannum reversus Pontanus, *Fol. page* 204. Constantius viginti una militum Britannorum millia sub Cassivelano, Guenone, et Guavara ducibus adduxit, *ibid. p.* 208. Aut Italiam populos aquilo genasque Britannas Ausonius Idill, *ibid. page* 752.

Eo nomine a Scotis et Britannis commerciis, frequentatam per Thormond. Torfæum, *Venlandiæ Antiq. Hist.* Quæ Regibus Britannis præducerat Merlinus, *Forcatulus de Gallorum imperio*, p. 459. Br. Mus. Insulis Britannis Thulen accensere Jonas Arngrimus Islandois Crymogea, homo Britannus loquens Richard viti ad Brotum, *page* 17. Certe publicus ordo principum Britannorum, *ibid. page* 122. Ex ordine publico Regum Britannorum, *ibid. page* 101. Quamobrem in

catalogo

catalogo Regum Britannorum de Libris Herculus patris hujus Galatii quos libros de Hiftoria principum Britannorum, *ibid. p.* 122. Crudeliffimam principum Britannorum, *ibid. lib. 7. page* 34.

Auguftinus Britannorum facerdotum auxilio deftitutus, *lib. 8. p. 72. ibid.* Et in ordine publico Regum Britannorum, *lib. 8. page* 77. Sociarumque virginium Britannarum fumpta, *Galfrido, page* 126.

So much for profe, in order to convince Mr. P. that *Britannus* is an adjective ; but what fhall we fay refpecting his fkill in poetry? Ah, and alas! it is to be feared that the fpecimen he has given of his abilities will place him very low among the old Romans. We fhall however make the trial on a paffage quoted by him from the verfes of the elegant Ovid, viz. *Vulgus adeft Scythicum bracataque turba Getarum trifte,* 111th Ultimo. But Mr. P. muft alfo correct him as well as B. by changing it to *vulgus adeft Scytharum bracataque turba Getarum.*

Thus, inftead of a dactyl having a long and two fhort in *A-deft Scy-thi,* Mr. P. has

made

màde it an Amphimacer, confifting of A-deft
Scy-tha, a long, a fhort and a long meafure.
Ah! alas! *Me miferum!* woe is me! Such an
outrage againft Ovid pleads more for compaffion than correction; we muft therefore inform him that A in the plural number of an
increafing noun is always long without
one exception to the contrary. *Vid. Rud.*
Profodia, Reg. 39. *pluralis cafus, fi crefcit*
protrahit A, E, et fimul O.

And here for his benefit we muft obferve,
that a fubftantive is ufed for an adjective, as
exercitus victor, pro victoriofo; and that
an adjective is fometimes ufed in the place of
a fubftantive, as fic poffum falli ut huma-
nus, pro ut homo; that the fingular is
fometimes taken for the plural, ut victor
Britannus fudit legionem, for Britanni victo-
res, the Britifh conquerors routed the legions;
et vice verfa, Tact. Annal. lib. 14. *cap.* 22.

We might point out that the abftract is
taken for the concrete, and the concrete for
the abftract; that the primitive is taken for
the derivative, and at times the derivative
for the primitive, the fimple for the compound,

pound, and the compound for the fimple.
But being noways inclined to become his tea-
cher, we fhall refer him to any fchoolmafter
of abilities for farther information, and there
he will find that any boy who will venture to
prefent his mafter with fuch an exercife, as
he has infulted the publick with in *Scytha-*
rum for *Scythicum*, will be moft heartily
flogged for his ignorance in hexameters.
And it is hoped that this leffon will render
Mr. P. more cautious with regard to his
future publications, in cafe any will be offered
to the publick, not knowing but that he
may meet with a fharper reproof from others
than the author choofes to give, fhould
people be troubled with more of his unfup-
ported and illiberal abufe of his fuperiors,
and fuch as never gave him any provocation ;
at leaft let him fpare the dead who cannot
reply or anfwer him.

THE END.